MONSTER OF THE LOCH

LUCAS PEDERSON

SEVEREDPRESS

MONSTER OF THE LOCH

Copyright © 2024 by Lucas Pederson

WWW.SEVEREDPRESS.COM

ISBN: 978-1-923165-26-7

OCTOBER 15TH, 1917

They found him, but how? He took all the precautions. Covered his tracks as best he could.

So how did they find him all the way in Scotland, of all places?

The ground crumbled under Dr. Pavel Gusev's feet, and he tumbled down a short hill to a narrow, stony shore where he lay panting. Everything hurt. Burned. The chilly, damp air made his lungs take on a slight raspy tone. Maybe if he lay here for a minute…they wouldn't notice him. Cold water licked his fingertips, startling him.

He sucked in a sharp breath and made sure the package he carried under his coat was safe. It was. Good. Very good. If it ever fell into the hands of the Soviet Union there would be horrors beyond imagination. Oh, how far they had fallen from what the Motherland was supposed to stand for.

Pavel stood. His raspy breaths puffed in front of his face like ghosts.

A large lake sprawled out before him. Loch Ness, if he remembered correctly. The shore, which was made up mostly of pebbles and rocks, stretched for what could be miles in either direction. He couldn't be certain, however. The fog from earlier appeared to be thickening. He could have sworn there was a bridge nearby. A road too. If he found either, they would lead him to the nearest town and relative safety. Maybe—

He heard the shot a second after a sharp pain lanced his right shoulder.

Pavel cried out, stumbled and fell to his knees on the wet, rocky shore of Loch Ness.

Rushed voices closed in. Someone else said, "Remember to secure the cargo. Do not kill the scientist."

Pavel, pain crashing through him from the bullet lodged in his right shoulder, managed a paper-thin chuckle.

He quickly brought out a fishbowl sealed at the top like a jar. Inside the bowl, Creation #4, or as he came to call it, Elle, swam around. It appeared to consider him for a moment before obviously taking in the new environment it saw through the glass. So intelligent for something so young. Only two weeks ago it was barely the size of a thimble. Now it stretched about seven inches long and had developed tiny flippers on the front and near what might be a tail later on in the aging process.

"There," one of his pursuers shouted.

Pavel glanced over his shoulder, heart bashing itself against his ribs. He looked at the fishbowl in his hands, at the tiny creature swimming around inside without a care in the world. Sometimes he wished he could be so carefree. He wished for peace.

"Stand where you are! Hands above your head!"

Pavel sighed. "I'm tired, Elle." The creature in the fishbowl paused as if it heard him.

"No talking! Hands above your head! Now!"

"So tired of running." Pavel drew his pistol.

"Stop talking! Turn around!"

"Alright," Pavel said. A tear streamed down his whiskered cheek. "Comrade."

Fishbowl tucked under his arm, Pavel swung around and fired two rounds into the nearest of his pursuers. The best the Red Army could spare to apprehend him and steal his Elle.

Pavel pointed his pistol at the next soldier and managed a single shot before a third soldier opened fire. Bullets pummeled into him, the force swinging him around like a horseshoe. At first, there wasn't any pain. Just a sudden loss of feeling. Strength leaked out of his legs and he fell to the stony shore of Loch Ness. The fishbowl shattered and the small creature flopped around between the rocks.

Pain exploded through Pavel as he reached for Elle. The loch's cold water lapped up the blood spilling out of him.

"Grab the creature!"

Pavel, crying out in pain, grabbed Elle and tossed her as far as he could into the water. She was made to survive every temperature, so the cold water didn't worry him. She was free now. Free to live.

The soldiers splashed through the water trying to capture Elle and Pavel smiled.

Gray waves crashed through him. His vision blurred.

"Be free," he whispered as his vision faded. "Live."

Then sweet, silent darkness consumed him.

NOW

1

"There it is." Jesse pulled back on the rod, body straining.

Becca joined him at the side of the boat with the net. "You see it yet?"

Jesse worked the reel for a bit then let the fish fight. He might have to let some line out if things got too crazy.

"Not yet," Jesse said and let out a little line to let the fish wear itself out. "Might be a muskie." He pulled back, reeled a bit, released a little line. The rod itself dipped in a heavy downward arc.

"Might be?" Becca said and chuckled. "I don't think a northern could do that."

Jesse snorted. "You've never had a big northern on the line then." He reeled in a bit. Pulled the rod back slowly. Reeled some more. The fish was getting tired now, though not enough to land it.

"I mean, I've had a couple big ones," Becca said.

"That's what she said," Jesse spouted and grinned.

"Hur-hur," Becca said. "Have I ever told you how shitty your jokes are?"

"You love it." Jesse pulled back on the rod and reeled the fish in a bit more. Wouldn't be much longer before it gave up. Hell of a fighter for a freshie, though.

Eventually, the fish rose to the surface.

"Muskie," Jesse said. "Gotta be a twenty pounder."

Becca lowered the net into the water and scooped the fish up. She swung it into the boat and unhooked it before Jesse could move. He smiled. They made a good team. Not so good romantically, but a good team, nevertheless.

Jesse secured the hook, placed his fishing pole in a holder and helped Becca lift the beast so they could measure and weigh it.

"Forty-three inches," Becca said and tossed the tape measure aside.

Jesse hooked the fish through the gills onto the weight scale.

Becca whistled. "You were close. Twenty-three point six pounds." The fish snapped its tail at her face. "Easy, lil'miss."

Jesse lit a cigarette and blew out a long jet of silvery smoke. "Hope you're hungry."

"Oh, we're eating this one?" Becca said and turned around. Her expression soured. "Thought you were going to quit."

Jesse grunted, took a drag, and slipped the cigarette into a half empty soda can. It hissed. He placed the can in a holder and nodded at Becca. "Been a stressful couple of weeks."

She frowned. "Not *that* stressful."

"I dunno," Jesse stowed the muskie in the live well of his boat and looked at her. "Losing Ray was pretty damn stressful."

Becca opened her mouth and closed it again. She nodded, face contorting a bit. "Yeah. He was a good boy."

The thought alone of ol' Ray brought tears to his eyes. All those days of playing fetch with a tennis ball or random stick. Swimming in the lake behind their cabin. Going on long rides in the truck. Snuggling in the warmth of the bed while winter raged outside...

Jesse sighed, shook his head and started the boat.

Becca lowered her head and sat down.

It wasn't her fault for drawing the memories back out to the forefront of his mind. She was just trying to help. He was the problem. He had always been the problem. That's why they could never be a couple, even though he loved her. It wasn't that he couldn't commit to her, it was the nightmares of kids exploding...of half of his best friend's head being sheared off by a fifty caliber round three feet away from him. The nightmares of war...

"You okay?" Becca said and Jesse blinked.

"Y-Yeah." He shook his head. "Let's head home and cook up that monster."

She smiled and nodded, though he could see it in her eyes. The hesitance. The concern. That was another reason they simply couldn't be. He couldn't have her looking at him like that every time he slipped into his thoughts. While fishing, he could avoid it better. But sitting at home doing normal family stuff...not so much.

PTSD was a bitch.

<u>2</u>

Jesse knocked back the rest of his beer, burped and stared out across Cass Lake. The sun was setting, and the water glowed in mellow pinks, reds and purples. He lit a cigarette and sighed.

Becca left about half an hour ago. The muskie was fantastic. Nice fried fillets for each and some fried potatoes to go with them. So good.

He missed her presence, though. Ray was the buffer for loneliness, and he was gone now.

Jesse cracked open another beer and took a swig. He smoked his cigarette and stared at the soothing colors shimmering on the lake. Somewhere nearby a loon called. It should be a personal paradise. That was the plan when he bought the place a few years ago. It was also the plan to replace Ray after he died. But now…now…

He couldn't fathom replacing ol' Ray. Maybe in a year or two, but not right now.

The sun sank behind the trees on the other side of the lake, dousing Jesse's tiny slice of the world in darkness. The sky sparkled with millions upon millions of stars. No moon tonight. He leaned back in his chair, crushed out his cigarette and sighed. He drank his beer. The crickets and frogs deepened their orchestra for the night. Bats squeaked, swooping to eat their fill of mosquitos. Speaking about mosquitos, the little bastards hadn't attacked him tonight for some reason. Not that he was complaining.

By all accounts, it was a nice evening. He just missed his dog.

Something scampered through the woods to the left of the porch. He had the gate to the porch locked and secure just in case a curious black bear wandered by. And if one got more than curious and tried to climb over…he had his twenty-gauge pump shotgun resting nearby. Those giant raccoons tended to surprise Jesse sometimes. That's what he tended to call black bears. Giant raccoons. Both critters are dumpster divers.

Jesse lit another cigarette. Yeah, he quit a few months ago. But damn it, he lost his dog. His best friend. Plus, the government was fucking him over on his VA benefits again. They supported the troops, sure, until those broken men and women returned from whatever conflict they were sent to. Then they didn't care and used veterans as pawns for political clout. It was disgusting.

He polished off his third beer of the night. The lake was a vast spread of darkness sparkling here and there under the starlight.

Around midnight, Jesse swayed and stumbled his way into the cabin. He locked the porch door and shuffled to his bedroom. His head swirled with the influence of twelve beers.

Jesse collapsed in his bed, rolled onto his side, and knew no more.

3

The next morning, he dragged himself out of bed around ten o'clock and made his way to the kitchen in his boxers.

He got the coffee pot brewing and opened the refrigerator. Beer took up most of the space. Not that he really drank that much, but it was good to have on hand for nights like last night. When the memories and the stranglehold of loneliness got too much, he needed a little something to keep the demons at bay.

Once the coffee was going, Jesse wandered to the bathroom, pissed, and took a quick shower. Dried off, he walked naked toward his bedroom.

"Whoa!"

Jesse sucked in a sharp breath and spun around, covering his genitals. "The fuck?" He reached for the pistol in the nearby desk drawer.

"It's just me," Becca said. "Sorry. Your door was unlocked, and I thought—"

"Jesus," Jesse said. He slipped behind the small China hutch his grandma gave him years ago. Even before Afghanistan. "I mean, there's a damn doorbell."

Becca chuckled. "Since when have I ever used the doorbell?"

He sighed. "Might start making it a rule now."

"Oh, it's not like I haven't seen it before."

"Don't say *that*," Jesse said, eyes widening. "You sound like my *mom*!"

Becca laughed and retreated to the kitchen. "Hurry up and get dressed so we can go."

A frown creased Jesse's face. "Go where?"

A loud clank, as if Becca dropped a pan. "Really?"

Jesse glanced around, mind reeling. "I…" Then it came to him. "Oh. Oh shit."

"You forgot?"

He cleared his throat. "No. I just…hey, you derailed my entire routine."

"Dude," Becca said and rushed out of the kitchen. "You know this is important to me." She glanced at his hands covering his male danglers then glared into his eyes. "You drank too much last night, didn't you…"

"What?" Jesse said and snorted. "No."

She frowned. "Liar. You rarely wake up this late."

Jesse sighed and waved a hand. "Okay, I had a couple."

"Of all nights," Becca said, expression darkening. "You chose last night." She turned and hurried out of the cabin.

He blinked, shook his head and ran a hand through his hair. "Shit."

4

Jesse pulled on a pair of jeans, slipped into a T-shirt, socks and tied on his boots. He stumbled out the door and onto the front porch, heart thrumming. Sure as hell Becca left him.

But her truck was still in the driveway behind his Jeep. She sat behind the wheel and glared at him.

He sighed, swept a hand through his dark hair and walked to Becca's truck. He got in and she started the truck without a word or a glance his way.

"I'm sorry," he said as she backed out of the driveway.

"That's nice," she said and put the truck into drive. "Now shush." She turned the radio up and they were on their way.

Jesse smiled and stared out his window. He felt like an asshole about forgetting what day it was.

A few miles through the woods, they emerged onto the highway and sped toward the town of Berry Mills. That would be the first stop. As they neared the town, Jesse already missed his tiny spot in the woods. Society always irritated him and spiked his anxiety. That's why he grew most of his own vegetables as well as hunted and fished for his meat. The less interaction with people...the better. No matter how lonely he got, Jesse simply couldn't be around people for too long.

Becca was the only person he enjoyed being around. And because of that, every year, he accompanied her on this day. She needed him and, truth be told, he needed her too.

About an hour on the road and they rolled into Berry Mills. He wanted a cigarette but managed to quell the urge with a piece of gum from Becca's center cupholder among the loose change and hair ties.

Becca stopped in front of Amy Rose's Flower Shop. She glanced at Jesse. "Be right back."

He smiled and nodded. "Yep."

Becca got out of the truck and hurried into the old flower shop. Amy had been in business since the sixties. Started it when she was only sixteen, too. If there was ever a saint, Amy Rose was one. Every year she donated a specific bouquet to Becca. One of the sweetest gestures Jesse had ever seen.

He thought about slipping out and smoking quick, but Becca came out with her large bouquet of yellow daisies, pink mums, with a splash of ferns. The same as it had been for years.

Becca placed the bouquet on the back seat of the truck and got in.

"All good?"

She nodded. "Like always." She rolled away from Amy's and back onto the highway toward their final destination.

Not far now, but his gum was beginning to get a bit stale and he really wanted a—

"Go ahead," Becca said and tapped the button to lower his window about halfway.

"Huh?"

"Oh, don't play dumb," she said. "I know you're craving a cigarette right now. You're all fidgety."

He snorted. "It's really that noticeable?"

"Uh, yeah." She waved a dismissive hand. "Hell, give me one too."

He gave her a double take. "Wait, what?"

She shook her head. "Knock it off and give me a fuckin' cigarette, already."

He brought out the hard pack of Marlboros and handed her one. She popped it between her lips, sifted through the center console and fished out a Bic lighter. Jesse blinked, not sure if he was seeing things or not. In the fifteen years he'd known her, Becca had never mentioned being a smoker before. She'd yell at him about smoking, of course.

Becca lit the cigarette and rolled her window down a bit. She blew out a jet of smoke.

Without looking at him, she said, "Not a word."

Jesse lifted his arms in surrender and lit his own cigarette.

They drove in silence and smoked. A little over five minutes, Becca crushed her cigarette out, coughed a little and sighed.

"I can't believe I did that." She rolled up her window.

Jesse flicked his cigarette butt out the window. "Yeah, well—"

"Hey," Becca said. "What the hell was that?"

"What was what?" He frowned at her.

"Dude." Becca pointed at his window. "You know how many forest fires are started by lit cigarette butts?"

Jesse chuckled and cocked his thumb at the scene outside. "That's a lake."

She blinked, rolled her eyes and returned her attention to the road. "Whatever. Don't throw your butts out the window like that."

He opened his mouth to make a joke and closed it again. Now wasn't the time for jokes. She was obviously on edge more than usual this time of year. Especially today.

"Okay," he said. "Sorry."

They rode in silence for a few miles.

Finally, Becca smacked the steering wheel with her hands. The truck swerved a bit.

"Whoa," Jesse said, holding on to what he always called the Oh Shit Handle, above his door.

She pulled over onto the shoulder, turned the truck off and got out.

Jesse blinked at the empty driver's seat for a handful of seconds and opened his door. He glanced out in time to see Becca walking through tall grass toward Acorn Lake. A lake locals claimed was haunted and plagued with deadly whirlpools which took the lives of many fishermen. Not that Jesse believed such stories, they were told often in the bars throughout the area. Especially by the older folks.

"Hey," he called after her and jumped out of the truck. "What's up?"

He rushed through the tall grass to a large sandy beach where Becca stood. She stared out over the water. Water, which, didn't appear clear. Water darker than he was used to. Colder…

A chilly breeze slithered over Jesse, leeching a shiver out of Jesse. The stories he heard about Acorn Lake wormed their way though his mind. He shook them off and looked at Becca. Her arms were crossed over her chest, attention fixed on the dark waters of the lake.

"Hey," he said, and glanced around. Suddenly he felt like he was being watched. Maybe the stories were true. Maybe evil entities really did dwell around the lake. "You okay?"

Becca sighed. "It gets harder and harder every year."

"Yeah," Jesse said and gently pulled her to him. She didn't fight him. He wrapped his arms around her in a loose hug and she leaned into him as they both stared out at the lake.

They stood that way for a few minutes and the eerie sensations worming through Jesse subsided. And that was okay.

He kissed the top of her head. "Ready?"

After a bit, she nodded. "Yeah, I guess."

They gave Acorn Lake a final glance and walked back to the truck.

5

Becca wiped a tear from her cheek and released a shaky sigh.

Jesse stood back a bit, but on standby. This was Becca's time, and he wouldn't interfere unless she needed him.

She lowered herself to her knees as a quiet breeze lifted her hair from her shoulders. She pulled the weeds growing around the black and white orb of marble stone. The stone itself was secured to a one foot by one foot granite slab. She placed a shaky hand on the marble orb.

"Happy birthday, sweetie." She sniffled and arranged the bouquet behind the marble orb. There was no sign of the bouquet from last year. "Been thinking a lot about you lately." She sighed and wiped tears from her face. "I miss you so much, Elle."

Jesse looked away. They were on a specific plot of forest Becca purchased after the tragedy happened. A warm summer breeze fluttered the green leaves of the trees surrounding them.

"Brought Jesse with me again," Becca said. "I know you liked him."

The breeze became a brief wind before settling down. If Jesse was a superstitious person, he'd almost believe Elle responded to Becca. But who knew for sure?

"I…" Becca sniffed. "I've had a pretty bad year, kiddo."

Jesse frowned. He wasn't hanging out with her every day, but she hadn't mentioned anything bad happening.

She wiped tears from her face and patted the marble orb. "Nothing I can't handle."

Jesse fought the urge to ask her why this year was so bad. What happened? But, he didn't have to ask.

"I lost my good job a couple of months ago, Elle." She sobbed a little. A very restrained sob. Just above a loud sniffle. Her entire body shook. After a few breaths, she lowered her head. "I'm broke and going to lose our house."

"Wait, what?" Jesse said.

But Becca ignored him. She was deep in it now. Something like a prayer, though not quite. A strong connection.

He lowered his head and waited. Minutes crawled by as she whispered to her dead daughter. Whispers so low he couldn't make out what she was saying.

Little Elle drowned years ago after some kid at her swimming lessons knocked her off the dock and into water well above her head. The swim instructor, who happened to be a Navy Seal veteran, hadn't noticed while he helped teach the younger kids the crawl stroke. By the time the instructor realized he was missing a child…it was too late. Becca spent a few days in jail for punching the instructor when she found out.

In all his time in the military, he had never seen a person break completely down over grief like Becca did. If Jesse hadn't been there for her, she might have followed little Elle to the grave. He hated to think about that, but it was true. He made her spend more than a few nights at his place so he could keep an eye on her and be there when she needed someone. A friend.

"I don't know what I'm going to do," Becca said, voice wavering just above a whisper. "But I know you're here. I *feel* you here." She shivered. "I love you so much, Elle."

Becca fell silent for a few minutes.

After a long sigh, she stood, wiped her face free of tears, and faced Jesse.

Hands clasped behind him, he smiled as best he could. "All done?"

She shivered, glanced back at Elle's grave, and nodded. "Yeah. I think so." She wiped away a stray tear and walked by him and onto the trail.

Jesse clenched his jaw and looked at the marble orb of Elle's grave. Another one of those warm breezes caressed his face and rustled the leaves. He closed his eyes, nodded, and smiled.

After a couple of minutes, he turned and joined Becca on the trail back to the truck.

6

They were about fifteen minutes from Jesse's home when he decided to broach the subject.

"Why didn't you tell me you lost your job?"

Becca's hands gripped the steering wheel for a moment, then loosened a bit. "I don't know."

"How much do you need to keep the house?"

She shook her head. "Nope. We're not doing this. Exactly why I didn't say anything. Not looking for handouts."

Jesse snorted. "Not offering a damn handout." He placed a hand on her shoulder. "Look, I'm here for you, no matter what. You know that."

The truck rumbled over the blacktop. Closer and closer to the gravel side road that would lead, eventually, to Jesse's cabin.

"I know," Becca said. "Why do you think I've wanted to go fishing so much this summer?" She laughed humorlessly. "Because fishing takes my mind off of everything."

"Aw," Jesse said. "And here I thought you enjoyed my company."

They rolled into Jesse's driveway, and she smiled. A genuine smile. "I guess I kinda like you too."

He chuckled and opened the door. "Wanna get a bite to eat and hit the water?"

"I mean," Becca said. "But looks like you already have some company." She pointed at his cabin.

Jesse frowned. He wasn't expecting anyone. But standing on his front porch was a man dressed in a black suit. He was maybe average height. Dark hair cut high and tight.

"There's a pistol in the glove compartment," Becca whispered.

"Good," Jesse said and got out. He looked at her before closing the door. "Use it if things look ugly then get the hell out of here."

She opened her mouth to respond but he closed the door before she could.

The man smiled and casually descended the porch steps to the flagstone walkway.

"Can I help you?" Jesse said, though remained near the truck.

"Mr. Robins?" the man said.

"Who's asking?"

The man stopped walking. His smile barely faltered as he spoke, which struck Jesse as a little creepy. "My name is Albert Cruse." He stepped closer and held out a well-manicured hand.

Jesse glanced from the hand to the man's face. "So? Why are you on my property?"

Albert chuckled and lowered his hand. "My apologies, Mr. Robins. My client asked me to come here on his behalf."

"Sure," Jesse said. "Who's your client?"

"Someone who has an...interest in a specific skill of yours." Albert grinned.

Jesse backed away a bit. "Who is your client and what skill are you talking about?" He glanced around. The tiny hairs on the back of his neck stiffened. His arms were littered in goosebumps. Something felt wrong.

"Why..." Albert slowly closed the distance between them. "Because you were considered the best fisherman in your unit."

Jesse frowned and opened the passenger door. "Sorry, Al. Not interested." He got into the truck, slammed the door and locked it. "Get the hell outta here."

When he didn't get a response from Becca, he turned his head and all the strength left him.

Instead of Becca, a tall, blond man sat hunched over the steering wheel.

Jesse opened the glove compartment and—

"Night, night…Mr. Robins."

A sharp pain pricked the side of his neck…

And he knew no more.

***

When Jesse opened his eyes, he found himself on a cot that couldn't be much larger than a bathtub. A low wattage lightbulb flickered near the door, which was shut.

His head throbbed and for a few minutes he just lay there staring at the ceiling.

Once his head stopped throbbing, he sat up and looked around. The room was utterly white and bare of furniture save for the cot he sat on. A vague aroma of vanilla touched his nostrils. He stood and walked over to the door.

Locked.

He took another look around. No windows. No vents that he could see. Just a small, white square room with a cot and a faulty lightbulb.

The doorknob rattled a bit and he backed away, hands clenched into fists. Whoever locked him up here was going to pay.

The door opened and—

"Hey," Becca said. She held a tray of food that reminded him of his middle school days. "How you feeling?" She was smiling. Which was even weirder.

"What…" He frowned, and tried to glance around her through the doorway.

She snorted. "It's okay. We're not in danger."

"We're—what the fuck? How are we not in danger?"

Becca placed the tray on his cot and smiled at him. "She told me she'd talk to you after you get some food in you."

"Who?"

"I'm not supposed to tell you."

Jesse rolled his eyes. "You gotta be fucking kidding me."

"It's nothing bad," Becca said. "Trust me."

"Trust you?" Jesse gestured at the small room they stood in. "This doesn't exactly exude trust!"

Becca smiled. "You'll see." He glanced at the food. "Eat up and meet us down the hall. The sixth door on the left." She paused. "You gotta eat, though. Otherwise, she won't let you in the room." And, with that, she walked away.

He frowned after her and shook his head. "What the hell is going on?"

He glared at the tray on his cot. The food…a cheeseburger, handful of thick steak fries, a cup of mixed fruit and a large tumbler of water…looked delicious. Especially with his stomach grumbling. Nothing like the slop the school fed him back in the day.

After a bit, he scarfed it all down. He stepped into the hall, still drinking water from the large tumbler. To the left of his room was a wall. To the right was a long hallway. Not quite large enough to be a corridor. He grunted and walked down the hall to the sixth door on the left. He took a swig of water from the tumbler and opened the door.

"Ah!" An older woman with short, silvery hair dressed in a black T-shirt and jeans stood from a table where several other people were seated. "There ye'are!" She sounded Irish. Or maybe Scottish? He wasn't quite sure.

He nodded. "Do I know you?"

The woman snorted and waved a dismissive hand. "Me? Nah, lad. Yer family."

Jesse blinked. "Uh…what? Family?" He chuckled and glanced around. "Okay, look, I need some real answers here." His gaze fell on the older woman. "Why did you forcefully bring me here?"

The woman chuckled. "Come now, lad." She moved closer to him. "Forcefully? Aye, t'was a bit dramatic. But ya wouldn't've come along if I asked nicely."

"You don't know that," Jesse said.

"Ah, laddy…" She smiled. "I do know."

Jesse gave her a withering look. "Who the hell are you?"

"Yer hearin' ain't good, aye?"

"My hearing is fine," Jesse said and glowered at her. "Enough. Who are you and what do you want?"

The woman sighed. Her smile melted away and she looked at him with genuine firmness. His grandma had that look. The look that told you to shut up and listen without telling you to.

"Fair'nough," the woman said. "M'name is Emma Dougal and ye'don't know me, aye. But we're cousins. Yer mum's side."

Jesse blinked. "No way…" His mom's maiden name was Dougal.

Emma's smile returned. "Aye."

He opened his mouth and closed it again, not sure what to say.

"Jesse," Becca said as she stepped away from the wall across the room. He didn't even know she was there until now. "This was the only way to get you here."

His heart damn near stuttered. "Wait...*you* were in on this bullshit, too?"

She smirked. "How do you think they knew they couldn't get you here on your own?"

He stared at her for a long time, heart aching. "You betrayed me..."

Becca laughed. "Oh, stop it. I didn't betray you."

"Then what the hell do you call it?"

She shook her head. "Just listen to her, Jesse. Please."

He glanced from Becca to Emma and back again. "No. I'm good." He turned and hurried out of the room.

He started down the hallway.

"Jesse," Emma said from behind him. "Yer an heir to a fortune."

Jesse stopped and faced her. "What are you talking about?"

The older woman smiled. "Jesse Robins..." She pointed at him for emphasis. "*Yer* an heir to a fortune, aye."

Jesse snorted. "Yeah, sure. Lady, I'm not even Scottish and you're wasting my time here."

He turned back around, ready to find his way out of whatever building they had him trapped in, when Emma said, "Aye, ya'are, Jesse. Yer mum was o'Scots descent."

"There was never any proof of that," Jesse said. Though a frown filled his face. He turned back to Emma. "She never got her ancestry report back. Some kind of mix up."

Emma, smiling, her blue eyes glimmering in the dim light of the hallway, said, "Nah there wannit a mix up, lad. Yer mum was in contact with m'uncle." Her smile was warm. Genuine. "Aye, yer family. Our clan."

He frowned. "Do you have any proof?"

"Aye," Emma said and gestured to the door of the room.

Once she realized he wasn't going in there first, she walked through the doorway. Jesse sighed, glanced down the hall, sighed again, and followed her into the room.

Emma sat at the table, smiling. Becca was seated beside her.

Eventually, Emma pointed at the far wall. "Watch."

From a ceiling projector, his mom popped onto the wall as a man dimmed the lights of the room. Instantly, his heart ached seeing her. He fought the tears threatening to blur his vision, though to no avail.

ALS was a bastard disease he wished he could annihilate instantly. No one should have to go through that kind of slow death.

His mom smiled at the camera, but Jesse felt like she was smiling at him. His heart ached even more. She appeared to be in the final stages of her life. Her gnarled, thin hands folded in her lap. Her face was gaunt, though not as skeletal as it would eventually end up.

Jesse wiped a few tears from his cheeks.

"Hi, Jesse," Mom said. Her voice was soft and full of warmth.

He nearly broke down right then. It had been years since he heard his mother's voice. Not that he could ever forget it, but hearing her out loud...

A warm hand clasped onto his own. Becca, standing beside him, smiled.

Jesse returned his attention to Mom projected on the far wall.

"I hope you find this video and understand why I kept our family history a secret." She sighed. "It was for your own safety, and I hope you understand that."

She smiled. "A copy of this video has been sent to a family member in Scotland, where our ancestors come from with the instruction for his niece, Emma, to show you in the event of his death. You'll love Emma, Jesse. She's a good one."

Jesse glanced at Emma, who stood behind him near the table. She simply smiled and pointed at the far wall.

"Jesse, since I'll be passing soon..." She needed to stop and take a few slow breaths. He longed for the warmth of her hug. "You are the heir to a Scottish fortune." She smiled and cocked her head to the side a bit. "I know you're skeptical, honey, but it's true." Her breathing was becoming labored. "Jesse...my sweet, handsome boy...I love you. If I can't say it before the time comes...I love you so much." Tears trickled down her cheeks and the video ended.

Jesse gasped, wiped his own tears from his face. He backed away, trying to let go of Becca's hand but she squeezed tighter.

"It's okay," she whispered.

He shook his head, and, knees quivering, plopped into the nearest chair.

On the far wall, his mother smiled at him, and he couldn't stop crying.

7

"I've booked our flight," Emma said while Jesse packed a suitcase with a couple of pairs of jeans, a few T-shirts, a couple of sweaters, socks and underwear. "We leave in two hours."

He zipped the suitcase up and nodded. "Okay. Let's go."

Emma chuckled. "Yer gonna wanna bring warmer clothes, lad. Gets kinda nippy where w'goin'."

Jesse grabbed another sweater and a jacket along with a beanie. He shoved them into the suitcase, zipped it up and turned to Emma.

"Better?"

She clapped him on the back. "Aye, lad. Aye."

They met Becca in his Jeep and hit the road.

"Slow down, dude," Becca said and laughed. "I don't think the money is gonna walk away."

He grunted. "In this day and age? Wouldn't surprise me."

"The fortune is safe, laddy," Emma said from the backseat. "Don't wanna end up a splattered egg outside m'own country."

"So, you'd rather be a splattered egg in your country?" Jesse said and chuckled.

"Aye," Emma said and winked at him in the rearview mirror. "I would."

Jesse slowed down a bit and let himself relax. It wasn't just the small fortune he'd inherited, though that played a major role in his excitement. It was also going to Scotland and seeing it for himself. It was one of the few places he had always wanted to visit. That and trying their beer. For some reason that was on the top of his bucket list, though not entirely sure why.

In about an hour, they arrived at the airport and checked in. About another half an hour later, they were on the plane.

A few minutes after takeoff…Jesse fell asleep.

8

Jesse sat in his chair, wishing he wore a jacket instead of a long sleeved shirt, while the man with the short gray hair behind a large wooden desk sifted through a few papers.

Seated next to him, Emma sighed.

"Git on'wit it."

The man, who only went by Mr. Toole and nothing more, sighed and leaned back in his chair. His steely gaze fixed on Jesse.

"Mr. Robins." Mr. Toole crossed his arms over his narrow chest. "I'm 'fraid I cannot allow transaction at this time."

Jesse frowned. "What? Why?"

"What's this, Mr. Toole?" Emma blurted. Her tone was as sharp as a keenly honed knife. "Yer o'bligated, ya know."

Mr. Toole's gaze drifted to Emma. "Aye, lass. T'ya." He nodded at Jesse. "Not this lad."

"This *lad*," Emma said, voice rising. She stood and pointed at Mr. Toole. "This *lad*, is the beneficiary, ye'toad!"

The man behind the desk blinked at her, obviously not used to a woman talking to him like Emma did. A dickhead, in other words.

After glowering at Emma for about a full minute, Mr. Toole waved a dismissive hand.

"Do ya have proof o'this lad?"

"Ya got it on yer bloody desk," Emma said.

Again, he waved a dismissive hand at her. "Nothin' solid, lass."

"There'r blood tests, Mr. Toole," Emma nearly shouted.

"Aye," Toole said. "B'how do I know it's this lad's blood?"

Jesse shot out of his chair, rolled up the sweater sleeve covering his right arm and leaned over the desk so Mr. Toole could get a good look.

"They jabbed me four times, asshole," Jesse said.

Mr. Toole frowned. His Scottish accent smoothed a bit. "Sit down, Mr. Robins, or I'll have ya removed."

Jesse plopped down in the chair with a heavy sigh and rubbed his temples. "I took all the blood tests, man."

"The tests." Mr. Toole chuckled humorously. "Aye. They're a match but'er they real?"

"The fawk ya mean now real, *Thomas*?" Emma shouted. "I watch'em *draw* the blood!"

Mr. Toole nodded. "Aye, so ya said." His glare sharped on her. "Don't call me Thomas." He stood and lit his pipe. The air soon wafted with sweet tobacco smoke.

Jesse always liked the smell of pipe tobacco.

Toole puffed a few times, drew the pipe away and blew a gentle stream of smoke. He pointed at Jesse with the tip of his pipe. "Ya think yer heir t'the McCombs fortune, aye?"

Jesse shrugged. "The blood tests match. That should be enough."

"Did ya ever know the man?"

Jesse frowned. "No, but—"

"Then the tests d'not matter, lad."

"The fawk?" Emma said. "Tests *do* matter, ya cunt."

Mr. Toole sighed and waved a hand. "B'gone, the both of ya." He turned and faced the only window in the stuffy office. He puffed on his pipe.

"Fuck you," Jesse said. He stood and upended Mr. Toole's desk, pinning the man to the window.

"Shit," Toole shouted, tried to turn around, though to no avail.

Jesse grabbed the papers from the desk and sifted through them. After a minute, he glared at the older man's back.

"You motherfucker. McComb even gave his blessing in that letter." Jesse kicked the desk, driving it into Mr. Toole even more. The man cried out in pain.

Emma pulled on Jesse's arm. "Come now, lad. He ain't worth spit."

"I'll have ya in jail," Mr. Toole said in a strained voice. "Both o'ya!"

"C'mon, lad," Emma said, still tugging on Jesse's arm.

Jesse clenched his jaw, righted the old lawyer's desk and walked out of the office without a word.

"Hey," Emma said, hurrying to catch up to him.

"I knew it was a bad idea to come here," Jesse said. Instead of getting into Emma's vehicle he decided to keep walking on the wet sidewalk toward the hotel.

The air was chilly with a light mist. He'd left his jacket the car and wore only a long-sleeved shirt and jeans. How far was the hotel? A few blocks?

"Jesse." Emma brushed up next to him and shoved his jacket at him. "Put this on right now b'fore ye catch yer death."

After a few seconds, he thanked her and slipped into his wool-lined jacket. They walked together for a few minutes. Vehicles trundled by. Somewhere nearby, kids were laughing. Other than the steely gray sky and misty air...Jesse kind of liked Scotland. Especially the town he walked in now, Inverness. It almost felt ancient or like he was in a random village in Lord of The Rings or something.

There was a magical quality to the town. Even the air felt magical.

All of that, however, didn't stop the rage bashing through his nerves. His heart thrummed.

"Ya might be put in jail t'night," Emma said.

Jesse nodded. "Not the first time."

She snorted. "Ya haven't been in a Scottish jail."

"I'm sure they're all the same."

"Aye, maybe." She cocked a thumb over her shoulder. "But ol'pisser back there'll make yer time hell."

"Been through worse."

"Yer mum said ya were military?"

He nodded. "Like I said…been through worse."

"Aye," Emma said.

They walked for another couple of minutes, not saying anything.

"So," Jesse said. "I might as well go back home, right?"

Emma didn't respond right away and when she did her tone was gentle. "Aye, ya can. But it might not be a good idea." She winked at him. "Mr. Toole can be a cunt, but there's a reason m'uncle chose'im to oversee the estate."

"What?" Jesse said. "You think he'll change his mind?"

She nodded. "Aye. Give'im a day'n a pint."

Jesse sighed. "Fine." He glanced around. "So…anything fun to do around here?"

Emma snorted. "Grabbin'a pint or two."

"Well…" Jesse smiled. "Looks like that's our afternoon sorted."

"Aye," Emma said and laughed. "Sorted."

SOMEWHERE ON LOCH NESS

Nobody bothered Norman much, which suited him just fine, thank you very much.

His little fishing boat rocked back and forth on the dark waters of Loch Ness. The mist ended a while back. Hour? Two hours? Hell, he couldn't remember.

He drank the rest of his beer, tossed the bottle into the Loch, and opened another bottle. He stared up at the night sky and smiled at the spray of glimmering stars. Lisa loved to look at the stars. God, he missed her so much. How long had it been?

"Six years," Norman said and wiped a few tears from his cheeks. "Miss ya, lass." He raised his bottle to the sky and spilled a bit of beer on himself.

"Ah, piss," Norman growled and sat up a bit.

He blinked and glanced around. He was surrounded by absolute darkness.

"Fuck," he said.

Unlike other nights, he forgot to anchor the boat and drifted deep into Loch Ness without a single light to guide his way back to shore. Of all the stupid things…

Norman lit a cigarette. There was no need to get excited. Loch Ness was big, but nothing like the ocean. Eventually, he'd bump into a beach. Then he'd walk back home. Would be shit coming back in the morning to get his boat, though, and—

Something thumped the bottom of the metal boat. A dull clunk.

Norman sat up a bit, heart thrumming. He glanced around and, of course, saw nothing but darkness. Water lapped against the sides of the boat. Other than that, the loch was quiet. Eventually, he chuckled and finished his cigarette. He tossed the butt into the loch and sipped his beer.

"Jus'o'log," He chuckled and swigged his beer. There were only two more left so he hoped the boat would drift to shore soon. He didn't want to row around the loch all night. He wasn't young anymore, after all.

"Young, heh," Norman said and drank his beer. "Not been young in a long time."

Time moved on and sometimes it caught people off guard. Sure as hell caught him off guard because—

Something struck the bottom of the boat again. Hard enough to rock the boat a bit.

"*Shit*," Norman shouted.

He scrambled around in the boat, heart slamming into his ribs.

"Not a log," he muttered and grabbed his flashlight.

Norman, breathing heavily, swept the flashlight back and forth over the water surrounding the boat. The beam only found wavy dark water. He ran a shaky hand over his sweaty face and released a nervous little laugh.

He moved the flashlight beam to the right and sucked in a sharp breath.

Just below the surface, large yellow eyes glared up at him.

"Holy mother'o'God," Norman managed and, still keeping the flashlight on the creature, slipped the oars into the slots on either side of the boat. "Gotta go now. Time ta'go."

Trembling, he tossed the flashlight on his lifejacket and sat on the center bench of the boat. He grabbed the oars.

Old Norman managed a single stroke before the monster rose out of the water, only faintly highlighted by the stars. A deep growl drained all the strength out of Norman. His hands fell away from the oars and the boat drifted a few feet before slowing to a stop. And, even in the gloom, he spotted those large yellow eyes.

It was true. All of it. The legend—

The monster lunged and snapped Norman up in its toothy jaws. Blood splattered in every direction and rained onto the boat. Norman released a wail of agony before the creature pulled him under into the cold, dark depths of Loch Ness.

The next day, Norman's old aluminum boat was found clunking and screeching against a rocky beach by a married couple out for a stroll.

The woman screamed when she saw all the blood splattered and pooled in the boat.

9

"Told ya the ol'cunt would come around," Emma said as she parked her vehicle in front of the large house of the late Mr. McComb.

Jesse snorted. "Yeah, you did."

"I'm still kinda pissed you guys didn't let me go too," Becca said.

"Because we knew you'd hurt the guy," Jesse said.

Emma smacked his arm. "Ya'bout crushed th'man with his own desk, lad."

Becca snickered. "I'm surprised he agreed to give you the keys to the place after that, dude."

Jesse shrugged. "Guess I made a different impression."

They got out of the car and stared at what Emma called the "McComb Manor". The place wasn't exactly a mansion by American standards, but large enough. A nice big brick house Jesse wouldn't mind living in. Well…that was if he wanted to live in Scotland, anyway. Which he didn't. He missed his little cabin by the lake already.

"So," Becca said. "You get *all* of this?"

"Nah," Jesse said and pointed at Emma. "She does."

"Aye," Emma said. "Be a good home f'm'family."

"Oh," Becca said and frowned.

Jesse chuckled and walked to the front door. "You'll see."

"I better not have travelled all this way for no fortune," Becca said and grinned. "You're supposed to be my sugar daddy now."

Jesse laughed while Emma opened the door. He leaned over and kissed Becca's cheek.

"Ew," Becca said and laughed. "Ask a girl out first, dickhead."

Together they laughed and stepped into McComb Manor. Honestly, Jesse felt good. He was getting a small lump sum of money that would help massively with fulltime retirement. Actually, as soon as he arrived in the United States, he was going directly to a financial expert to get everything legally sorted and set up for retirement.

The inside of the house smelled vaguely of either cigar or pipe tobacco and what could be vanilla, though Jesse wasn't sure.

"Wow," Becca said, eyes widening.

"M'uncle was a class all'is own," Emma said and smiled.

Jesse nodded. "This is nice."

"Aye."

They walked around the first floor for a bit, but Emma quickly led them to the second floor. After a quick glance at the six bedrooms, they came to a large set of wooden, ornate doors. The carvings in the wood intrigued Jesse. They were beautiful, though seemed haunted in a way. Dark. He traced what appeared to be some kind of snake-like creature.

"M'uncle was a bit'obsessed wi'Nessie," Emma said.

"Nessie," Jesse mused. "The Loch Ness Monster."

"Aye," Emma said and chuckled as she opened the doors. "He believed it't'be real."

In front of Jesse the study sprawled out in all its library-like glory. Indeed, it was nearly as large a damn library too. Books lined the walls all the way to the ceiling. Jesse wasn't a big reader but enjoyed a good book now and then.

Toward the far end of the study a massive wooden desk dominated the view. Like a slumbering beast.

Jesse couldn't stop staring at it. The thing was beautiful.

"The funds'll be in yer account in a few days," Emma said. She swept a hand at the study. "Everything here is yers too, lad."

Jesse blinked. "Everything?"

"Aye."

"Welp," Becca said and looked at Jesse. "You bring the U-Haul?"

Jesse laughed and walked to the desk. The legs were intricately carved, but he wasn't sure what they were depicting. They had a serpentine shape to them, though. Like snakes crawling up the desk's legs. The top was a large, polished slab of what Jesse assumed was oak. The entire thing had to have cost a small fortune itself.

"Uncle McComb loved art," Emma said beside him. "Wood art, 'specially."

"I see that," Jesse said and walked around the desk. The fingertips of his right hand slid over the monstrosity's edge. He rolled the black leather chair back, sat down, and for a moment got to see what his deceased relative had seen. The gorgeous, sprawling study.

He leaned back in the chair and inhaled the ghosts of pipe smoke. There was also a hint of cedar flirting with the ghosts and for a minute, he could see himself living here. He could envision himself sitting behind the beautiful desk in the beautiful study and writing his first novel or simply enjoying the quiet.

Becca and Emma smiled at him.

"Look at you," Becca said. "Like one of those sophisticated professors, or something."

Jesse rolled his eyes and waved her off. "Shut it." He pulled open the long center drawer of the desk.

The drawer had a small stack of Post-it notes, pads, a few pens and on the right was a black leather bound journal with the initials E.M. Edward McComb. He brought the journal and placed it on the desk.

"Aye. N'avid journalist, m'uncle was." Emma grunted and glanced around the study. "He nev'let anyone in here."

"So," Becca said. "How are we getting everything back home?"

Jesse shook his head, opened the journal and closed it again. It felt like invading someone else's privacy.

"Nah," Emma said. "He stated yer s'posed t'read th'journal, lad."

Jesse frowned. "That's weird." He looked at the journal. "Why would he—"

"Best t'just read it, Jesse," Emma said and chuckled. "Yer welcome t'stay th'night'r'two."

"Really?" Becca said. "Me too?"

Emma clapped Becca on the back. "Aye, lass. Food in th'fridge downstairs. Rooms'r'well furnished."

"Wait," Becca said. "You planned all of this?"

Emma snorted. "Well, o'course." She turned and walked to the door of the study. "I'll be back in the morn'." She walked out before Jesse could say goodbye.

Neither Jesse nor Becca said anything until the front doors opened and clapped shut.

After a moment, Becca sat in one of the chairs in front of the desk. "Dude...this is amazing."

Jesse nodded. "Yeah, it is." His fingertips traced the E.M. on the journal. He took a long look around. "I don't think half of this will fit in my cabin."

"Hell," Becca said and laughed. "Not even a quarter will fit."

He smiled and nodded. After a bit, he gestured at the room. "So, what the hell am I gonna do with it all?"

She shrugged. "I dunno, dude. We have like twenty-four hours left for you to figure it out and I'm starving."

Jesse broke out in a bit of laughter and stood. "Let's go see what they left us in the fridge."

10

After stuffing their faces with steak and potatoes Emma had left for them in the fridge, something Jesse wasn't expected but delighted to see, Becca said she wanted to relax a bit and watch some Scottish TV. There was only one TV in the house and it wasn't in the living room, but in a smaller less furnished room away from the living room. Like it was some kind of castoff forgotten thing.

Jesse decided he wanted to check out the study some more. Especially that journal. Why would Edward McComb want him to read it? Weren't journals, like diaries, personal? Or was it different in Scotland?

He sat in the chair behind the beautiful monstrosity of the desk, picked the journal up, and leaned back. A folded sheet of paper fell into his lap when he opened the journal. A frown touched his face as he returned the journal to the desk and opened the sheet of paper.

Jesse's frown deepened as he read.

Dear Mr. Robins,

Hello there! I know we have not met, but lo and behold here we are. Me talking to you through this old sheet of paper as my life has no doubt expired by this point. Thank your wonderful mum for all of our glorious chats. She was quite the woman, as you know. I was delighted to find out I had a relative from across that old pond. She is a blessing.

I know this all may come as a shock. The money and this study. But here is something I dared not put in my will or that cranky old Mr. Toole would have jumped on it like the toad he is. This journal is, at first, the translation of another journal I acquired years ago.

An older journal, which you find in the bottom right-side drawer of the desk. It is frail, so please handle it with the utmost care.

By now, I am sure my lovely niece, Emma, has told you about my interests in Nessie. Although I loath that name...because it is not her real name. But Nessie works so you know what I am talking about. You see, not only have I seen the creature a few times, I know of its origins. I also know how Scotland is covering up for its yearly rampages. Which is coming up here soon. A time when Loch Ness and Loch Morar will be extremely dangerous. I believe there are tunnels connecting the lochs.

Anyway, it is all in the journal there. I implore you to read it in one night. It is not very long. My real journal has already been burned. My life is like ashes, so they say. Too much for this small town to handle if ever read.

Jesse blinked at Edward's signature for a full minute before leaning forward and placing the letter on the desk. He bent and fished out a box from the bottom right drawer. Inside the box was a tattered and bloated journal. Also, leatherbound, though torn and scarred, barely held together by a weathered strap.

Carefully, he brought out the old journal and gently opened the rusty clasp holding it all together. It puffed open. Its pages, some of them loose, were dry and crackly to the touch. He opened it to the first page.

It took him a bit to get through some of what just appeared to be random chicken scratch.

"Russian," Jesse whispered. He recognized some of the lettering, though never learned the language.

Jesse reclasped the journal, slid it aside and picked up Edward McComb's. Once more, he leaned back in the chair and began to read.

For Jesse Robins, the dedication read. *What follows is a translation of the journal from the lower right drawer of the desk. Yes, it is Russian, or at the time it was written, Soviet Union. The name of the man who owned the journal is Dr. Pavel Gusev. A Soviet Union scientist and geneticist. I saved time by not translating his personal life and focusing it more on his studies. Time is of importance too, Mr. Robins. Please read swiftly.*

Jesse glanced at the old Grandfather clock in the corner. It was almost seven o'clock in the evening. He flipped through the journal and sighed. It wasn't long, but it would probably take him all night to finish.

"Fuck it," he said. "Nothing better to do anyway."

It wasn't just that, though. He was kind of intrigued. What was so important that McComb needed Jesse to know?

Jesse flipped to the first page, which was titled: Dr. Pavel Gusev.

We are heading into new discoveries today. I hope. A breakthrough in the splicing will keep Ivanov off my back for another week. Perhaps.

On the far right of the page, McComb added: Ivanov was Pavel's boss. A government official overseeing the genetic splicing program Pavel ran.

Jesse continued reading.

Though he does not know about my secret project. This project is one I wish to impress Ivanov with the most. The cell splicing appears to have taken hold nicely and I will be observing its growth. Early stages yet without recognizable growth. The cells appear to be multiplying, which pleases me. Will keep this journal updated as the experiment progresses.

Jesse flipped to the next page and entry.

Had to leave home early today and get a jump on the testing results due tomorrow. Not for my secret project, but for the bear research. The government wishes to create a species of bear with a thick hide like an elephant and the size of the extinct short-faced bear. They want to use the animals during times of war to scare and maim enemies. If not to distract. They would be our Kamikazes, I suppose. Horrifying to think about. But I must do what I must do.

Jesse turned the page to a new entry, which was about a week from the last one.

The secret project is growing! Yes. The cells formed an embryo. The next phase I will secure it in an aerated container and attach a feeding tube. I suppose I must say what my secret project is. Although, if this journal is ever found I will surely be tortured for information and quickly dispatched. Regardless, I feel I owe it to myself to reflect on my achievement. The project is an ambitious one and could terminate at any time now.

It all began with a single mosasaurus cell being added to a plesiosaur. Both cells were extracted from recently discovered fossils. To strengthen the genetic codes, which I could only guess at as much as this work is trial and error rather than knowing anything, I added in a mix of cells from a cuttlefish for the ability to camouflage and intelligence, and Greenland shark to be able to adapt in colder water. I, for one, never thought the cells would interact and multiply to form an embryo. Bye for now, as I must get to work.

The Grandfather clock in the corner chimed, startling Jesse. He sat up, stretched and squinted at the clock.

"Holy shit," he said. "It's already been an hour?" He flipped through the journal.

Jesse stood, stretched, and sat back in the chair. Pavel's journal was dated during the year 1917. Which would have been around the time of World War I, if Jesse remembered his history right. Still, it read like a late 1950's science fiction story. Did they even have the technology for genetic splicing back in 1917? If so…that changed everything. Maybe it wasn't actual splicing but more like just tossing cells together and seeing what happened? That sounded closer to what Pavel was talking about.

Jesse skimmed over the next entry, but it was much of the same. The following entry, however…

I have successfully attached an umbilical feeding tube to the embryo and will be feeding it nutrients that I hope will lead to life beyond the embryo phase. I cannot believe the experiment has made it this far. A breakthrough! My fourth attempt was a success! So far. Perhaps it is too early to celebrate, but I think Creation #4 will finally be the breakthrough I needed. We can, indeed, use ancient cells to create a new species. The information will aid us in the next phase of the bear project. I couldn't be happier than I am today.

Jesse turned to the next entry which was about a month from the last one.

I'm in danger. I think Ivanov knows about Creation #4. Experiments not of his knowledge could be terminated. I watch Creation #4 right now on my break while I write this. She…yes, I believe it is a female, swims in the fishbowl. Only a little over two inches, she runs into the glass repeatedly. She needs a name, I think. Elle. I will name her Elle. I should not get attached, but…

Jesse blinked and placed the journal on the desk.

"Elle," he said, thinking about Becca.

Taking a break from the journal, Jesse ventured downstairs to the TV room where Becca was fast asleep on the couch. He smiled, pulled the blanket up over her shoulder and turned the TV off. He walked around the first floor a bit and found himself in the spacious kitchen. It was hard to believe one person lived in such a large place alone.

Jesse made himself a ham sandwich, grabbed a bottle of water, and returned to the study.

DORES BEACH, LOCH NESS

The small rocks and sand crackled under their shoes. Above, the moon was but a thin sliver of light surrounded by darkness. Crickets chirruped from the woods. The dark waters of Loch Ness washed over the rocks.

Amy swept the flashlight back and forth.

"I don'think we'll find any," Caleb said and swept his own flashlight.

They weren't supposed to be out here this late at night, but when Amy had an idea, she always followed through. Even if the idea turned out empty.

Like tonight, if Caleb was to be honest.

"Hush," Amy said. She paused; flashlight focused on a large rock. After a minute or so, she moved on.

Caleb sighed. He checked the time on his phone. Sighed again. They had been out here for almost two hours and it was damn near midnight. The air was damp and cold, and Caleb thought about leaving her and going home. The idea of his warm bed trumped walking on the old cold beach at midnight. And he would have done just that, except…she'd be out here all alone. She was his best friend and he couldn't just leave her like that.

"I hear yer sighs," Amy said. "Best we leave then."

"Aye," Caleb said and shivered. "Gettin'a wee bit nippy."

Amy swept the flashlight back and forth for another five minutes or so, then stopped and shrugged. "Too cold for frogs, I guess."

"Coulda tol'ya that," Caleb said and chucked. His teeth chattered.

Amy snorted. "Aye." She turned back in the direction from which they came. "Let's get home."

"'Bout fawkin' time."

They walked in silence for a bit.

Caleb was about to ask her if they were going to gather some mates tomorrow and play some D&D when a large splash came from the loch to their left. They stopped walking.

"Ya hear that?" Amy said.

"Aye." Caleb shivered. "Let's go."

"Could be Nessie," Amy said and giggled.

Caleb, having grown up hearing horror stories about the Monster of the Loch, Nessie, didn't laugh. His heart thundered.

"Let's go," he said and pulled on her arm.

"I'm goin', I'm goin'," Amy said and matched Caleb's quick pace.

Subtle splashes from the Loch. Almost stealthy. Small waves lapped at the beach.

Their pace quickened. Something didn't feel right. The air seemed thicker. The crickets stopped chirruping. The water sloshed along the beach.

"I don'like this," Caleb said.

"It's...it's just a seal in the Loch," Amy said. "It just—"

A deep growl shivered the cool air. Caleb stopped but Amy shoved him.

"Don'stop," she said. "Run."

Caleb was about to ask why when she shoved him again.

"Go!"

He started out in a sprint when a massive splash stopped him. He skidded on the wet rocks and fell hard on his butt. Amy screamed.

Scrambling to his feet, Caleb spun around. The beam of his flashlight caught a glimpse of a creature and Amy dangling from its massive jaws. The top half of her was in the monster's mouth while her legs kicked the air inches from the creature's long neck.

Caleb sucked in a sharp breath. His bladder let go, soaking the front of his jeans.

The monster thrashed, severing Amy's body in two. Her bottom half, legs still kicking, flew to the side and disappeared into the darkness. Blood rained down onto the beach. Her intestines tumbled out and made a wet, meaty smack on the rocks.

Every nerve in Caleb told him to run, yet his legs didn't move. His knees trembled. All he could do was gape at the massive creature while it swallowed down the top half of his best friend.

Then the monster's shiny yellow eyes shifted and fixed on Caleb.

He screamed, spun, and ran as fast as his legs would carry him.

He didn't look back…and couldn't stop screaming.

11

The last line from Pavel's journal read: *We leave for Scotland tomorrow...*

Jesse lowered the journal and glanced around the study. His gaze happened on the Grandfather clock. A little after midnight. He'd been reading for about two hours and still had McComb's addition. About ten more pages or so. He drank some water, stood and stretched. After a bit, he walked around the study.

The sheer number of books held him rapt for a while. Books all the way to the ceiling. Some fiction, others nonfiction. A large array of subjects and titles from what he glanced over.

"Imagine having the time to read all of these books," he whispered to himself.

He wasn't downplaying it, but kind of romanticizing it. Time was on his side, and he could see himself relaxing at home reading book after book.

Jesse returned to the desk and read Edward McComb's entries.

Those were Dr. Pavel Gusev's final entries. I bet you are questioning how any of that could be possible. Yes? The combining or splicing of cells was unheard of in the early 1900s. Yet, Pavel said they were doing just that during World War I era. If what he claimed in his journal was true or not...that's up for debate. But I will say this...Elle is real.

Jesse turned the page, frowning.

I have seen the creature a few times, although I believe it is not exactly Elle. Surely an offspring. The pictures are in an envelope taped at the end of this journal. But that is not everything I want you to be aware of. As I mentioned before, I will call her Elle II returns to Loch Ness every year at the same time of year. When she does...people go missing. It is now May 21st as I write this. Elle II will return in June. That's when people will go missing and sightings will occur. The town and locals will cover it all up, as they have for decades. They do this to keep Elle II safe, though not for any reason you may think. Most of them believe the creature was sent by God to protect them. Delusional thinking. I, too, believed this at one point. That was, until I translated Pavel's journal. Then it all made more sense.

Jesse nodded. As strange as Pavel messing around with cells and DNA back in the early 1900s was...the creature being sent by God was less believable. It played with the frayed ends of sanity. McComb was right. Delusional thinking.

Now, I want to let you in on the real reason you're here, Jesse. You see, your mum told me about your military achievements, and I got an idea. You may not like this part, however.

I want you to kill the Loch Ness Monster.

Jesse lowered the journal. A frown creased his face. What the hell did his mom get him into? He returned his attention to the journal.

Yes. You read that right. I want you to kill the Loch Ness Monster. Nessie. Elle. Elle II. Whatever. Now...I bet you are wondering why I would tell you to do such a thing. Understandably so. And here is the answer, twofold: Because she ate my granddaughter, and she is breeding. Thus, why there are sightings of similar creatures around the world. If allowed to continue breeding she might change the natural order of things. Imagine thousands of large creatures, at least the size of a humpback whale, eating all the natural predators in the oceans and becoming the apex predator. The more they breed, the worse for our fish populations and soon the demise of our oceans.

"Damn," Jesse said and tossed the journal onto the desk.

It was almost 12:45 now and he was getting tired. He wondered what room he would choose to crash in for a minute or two...then continued reading.

Do not think I am a heartless man, Jesse. I am not. Elle was a special creature. A scientific breakthrough. No doubts there. But Elle II must not remain living, nor should any of her offspring. Thankfully they are slow breeders otherwise I would not be writing this, and the world would be hurting. Ocean ecosystems obliterated. Now...here are my stipulations.

Jesse frowned. "The hell? Stipulations?"

If I were you, I would be curious. Yes?

"Uh," Jesse said. "Yeah. What the fuck?"

But let me assure you, Jesse, Mr. Robins...I will make this endeavor worth your while. Oh, Hell, that sounds like I'm some kind of mob boss from America. Anyway, I am willing to add an extra twenty million dollars to the five million already transferred to your bank account. Everything is set up and ready to go with Mr. Toole. He knows the details and stipulations. The moment Elle is put down and Toole shown the evidence, he will transfer twenty million dollars into your account. A large boat and small crew will be provided, as well as an array of weapons and traps. Your mum said you love to go fishing. Well, think of this as a special fishing trip. Okay, I know it is not a fish, but you get the idea.

Jesse sighed. "Yeah. I get it." He rubbed his closed eyes and yawned. "Twenty million bucks," he mused. After a minute or two, he finished reading.

Of course, the choice is yours and if you decline, you will still keep the funds in your account and our dealings will be sealed. Mr. Toole will burn this journal so there will be no ties to the creature and yourself. Mr. Toole will provide one way plane tickets back to the United States and that will be that. The choice is yours, Jesse. Either way…godspeed. Dearly Yours, E.M.

Jesse closed the journal and placed it on the desk. He leaned back in the chair and stared at it for a long time. He wasn't even sure what to think right now. His brain was a sluggish mess after all of that. Plus, it was almost one o'clock in the morning.

He stood from the desk and shuffled out of the study to the nearest room. He managed to kick his boots off before collapsing onto one of the softest beds he had ever felt. Jesse was asleep before he could get the blanket over his shoulders.

12

They were just sitting down for some coffee when Emma burst through the kitchen door.

Both Jesse and Becca stood but Emma rushed by them to the cupboards above the counter. She brought down a bottle of what looked like Scotch, poured a bit into a shot glass, and knocked it back.

"Emma?" Jesse said. "You—"

She held up a silencing finger, poured another shot of Scotch, knocked it back and slammed the glass down. She turned to them, tears trickling down her rosy cheeks.

"It's happening again," Emma said after a bit, barely choking out the words.

"What?" Becca said. "What's happening again?"

Jesse blinked. "Nessie…" He said it before Emma could open her mouth to reply. She stared at him and wiped tears from her cheeks.

"Wait, what?" Becca said. She glanced from Jesse to Emma and back again. "Nessie? Like the Loch Ness Monster Nessie? That Nessie?"

"Uck," Emma said, poured another drink and plopped down at the kitchen table. "Aye, sounds mad doesn't it?"

"Yeah, it does," Becca said. She frowned at Jesse. "Am I missing something here?"

"Remember McComb's journal?" Jesse said and sat at the kitchen table next to Emma.

"Yeah? So?"

"So…I was up reading it most of the night. He translated a little from a Soviet Union scientist who allegedly created the Loch Ness Monster."

Becca blinked. "The Loch Ness Monster? You're serious?" She glanced at Emma. "Both of you?"

Emma nodded. "Aye. I am. Seen it wi'me own eyes many times'n it's returned to the Loch."

Jesse sighed. "It's June."

Again, Emma nodded. "Aye. The killin's begun."

"Killings?" Becca said, eyes widening. "What are you two talking about?"

Jesse stood from the table. "I'll show you."

He led her to the study and handed her the journal. "Read it. I'm gonna talk to Mr. Toole."

She frowned at him. "Mr. Toole? Why? I thought—"

He tapped the journal. "Just give this a read and you'll understand." He walked toward the door. "I'll be back soon."

Jesse left her alone in the study, and motioned for Emma to follow him. He felt like time was of the essence now. Even if he only mildly believed the monster existed.

When they got into Emma's vehicle, she said, "M'niece is missin'." She started the car. "Could be Elle."

"Could be," Jesse said as she shifted the car into gear.

She nodded. "Y'read the journal. Y'know m'uncle left me one too." Before Jesse could speak, she lifted a silencing hand. "Don't wanna know what he wrote to'ya."

"All I'm going to say," Jesse said, "is I'll help as best I can and I'm sorry for your loss."

Emma smiled. "Aye. Thank you. She was a good lass. Adventurous. Reminds me o'me when I was younger."

Jesse nodded. With Emma's niece missing, it made everything a little more personal. A little more real.

When they entered Mr. Toole's office, the man himself was taking a nap on his couch across the room. He snorted, sat up a bit and glowered at Jesse and Emma.

"The hell y'doin?"

"I read Edward McComb's journal," Jesse said.

Mr. Toole's bushy gray eyebrows rose. "Oh? Is it so?"

"Yes."

The old man nodded, sat up, and slipped his round lensed glasses on. They slid down his hawk-like nose a bit and he pushed them back up with an index finger. He stood, straightened his suit a bit and looked at Jesse.

"Ya have the journal then?"

Jesse blinked. "Well, no. It's back at the house."

"Ah," Mr. Toole said and walked to his desk. "Pity."

"What do you mean? McComb said you were fully aware and onboard with everything."

Toole nodded and sat behind his desk. He leaned back and steepled his fingers over his chest. He glowered at Jesse.

"P'eraps I am, Mr. Robins." He sighed. "D'ya read the very las'page?"

Jesse frowned. "Yes. Ended with McComb saying Godspeed."

"Wrong las'page, Mr. Robins."

"What the hell are you talking about?" Jesse had never wanted to punch a man so much than he did right now. "That's the last page, asshole."

Toole snorted and leaned forward. "No, y'arse. The las'page is at the back o'the journal."

"Are you kidding me?"

"No, Mr. Robins." Mr. Toole leaned back in his chair again. "Go read it n'come back. Bring the journal w'ya."

"Uck," Emma said. "We're naw goin'back for the fawken journal."

"If ya wan'me t'help…ya better." Mr. Toole waved a dismissive hand at them.

Jesse chuckled humorlessly and moved toward the desk.

"Assault me again, Mr. Robins," Toole said, "n'I'll get ya deported."

Jesse stopped about two feet away from the man's desk, brought out his phone and smiled. "Don't worry…I'll phone a friend."

Mr. Toole frowned and cocked his head to the side a bit. He didn't say anything but Jesse could see the curiosity in his eyes.

Jesse called Becca. She didn't answer after the first series of rings. He hung up. Mr. Toole smiled.

"Issues?"

Jesse rolled his eyes. "Hold on." He was about to call her again when Becca's name popped up on his screen for an incoming call. He answered. "Hey."

"Everything okay? I was just reading—"

"All good. Hey, can you flip to the very last page of the journal and read it to me?"

She paused. The sound of pages flipping whispered in his ear for a few seconds.

"Okay," Becca said.

Jesse put her on speaker phone.

"You there?"

"Yep," Jesse said. "You're on speaker so Mr. Toole knows I'm not lying."

Mr. Toole's bushy gray eyebrows knitted together in a frown.

"Okay," Becca said. "So, it's a single sentence." She paused. "Tell Mr. Toole he's an arse for making you read this sentence."

Jesse blinked and looked at Mr. Toole.

Mr. Toole raised one of his bushy eyebrows.

"You're an *arse* for making me read this sentence."

Toole shook his head. "Y'din't read it."

"Oh, f'fawksake," Emma spouted. "Stop yer shit."

Mr. Toole chuckled and kept his attention on Jesse. After a minute or so, he held up his hands and chuckled. "Alright, then. Y'got me."

"Got you?" Jesse hung up on Becca. Probably hear about that later. "You mean you were messing with us this entire time?"

Mr. Toole stood, all of that grumpy old man persona melting away from him. He smiled and his face appeared to change a little. Not much, but he reminded Jesse more of a grumpy grandpa now than a mean old miser.

"Mr. Robins," Mr. Toole said and walked over to a large black safe in the corner near his desk. "I have a few things for ya." He turned the combination lock and glanced over his shoulder at Jesse. "Bes'ides what ol'Eddie told ya in that journal."

Jesse looked at Emma. She shrugged.

Mr. Toole opened the safe and brought out a small, white envelope. He closed the safe, spun the combination wheel and turned to Jesse.

"From yer mum." He held the envelope out. When Jesse didn't take it right away, the older man smiled. "Come now, lad."

Jesse blew out a heavy breath and took the envelope from Mr. Toole. The old man moved away and sat behind his desk.

"Take all'th'time y'need, lad," Mr. Toole said.

Jesse opened the envelope and pulled out a single sheet of notebook paper. Emma took the envelope away from him before he dropped it. It had been over three years since his mom passed away and seeing her elegantly scrawled handwriting again drained all of the strength out of him. He plopped down into the chair in front of the desk and read the letter. It wasn't long but tore open the old wound in his heart.

Hi Jesse,

If you're reading this letter, then you accepted Edward's proposal to destroy the creature. You're currently out on a fishing trip in Canada while I'm writing this. I'm glad you agreed, sweetie. It's important to stop it before things get out of hand. As Edward surely left for you in his journal, there are already a few descendants roaming different parts of the world now. I just wanted to leave this letter to tell you, if I don't get the chance, how proud I am of you. And that I love you so very much, Clinky.

Jesse wiped a few tears from his cheeks. Clinky was her nickname for him. She never gave him a reason why. Just what she called him.

I have to stop writing now because my hand isn't working right. It's advancing fast now, the ALS. I am going to miss you so much and never think I'm not watching over you in some way.

Love, Mom

Jesse lowered the letter and Emma handed him a tissue. He wiped his eyes, blew his nose and tossed the used tissue in the trash basket on the right side of the desk. He folded the letter up and sighed.

"Well, you made me cry," he smiled at Mr. Toole. "Thanks, asshole."

Mr. Toole snorted. "Aye. Yer welcome." He lit his pipe, puffed on it a bit and nodded at Jesse. "I have a small crew ready for ye."

"Yeah, Edward mentioned something about a crew."

Toole nodded. "Aye. Small'un. Got ye'a modest boat'n'supplies too."

Jesse chuckled. "This is like a mobster meeting or something."

Emma laughed and clapped him on the shoulder. "Yer lookin'at the Scottish Don, Jesse."

Mr. Toole rolled his eyes and made a shooing gesture. "Git'out with ye."

Jesse shook the man's hand and got the directions to where he would meet his crew.

"Good luck, Mr. Robins," Mr. Toole said. "I'll be here when yer done."

13

"What I don't get," Becca said as Emma drove them to the south docks of Loch Ness. "How were people reporting sightings of this thing even before World War One?"

"Aye," Emma said. "Tricky, in'it?" She sighed. "There be lots'o'stories. Lot'o'em just folk seein' things. Some, though…might be true. Not Nessie, but…somthin'…"

"Could have been seals or whales," Jesse said.

"Aye. A small whale or two popped in the loch every now'n'then. Seals too."

"So," Becca said. "All of those accounts before this thing escaped were just misunderstandings or people jumping to conclusions?"

"Aye. From what m'uncle has said and what I've picked apart from local folk."

Becca shook her head. "I don't know. Not sure I'm falling for all of this."

"Guess we'll see for sure or not," Jesse said.

A while later, they arrived at the southern docks of Loch Ness. There were only a few boats tied to the docks, but only one drew Jesse's eye. A large white one that reminded him of both a yacht and a large fishing charter. It was about the size of a yacht too. Well, give or take a few feet either way.

The crew Mr. Toole mentioned turned out to be larger than Jesse imagined. A dozen people from what Jesse counted as they readied the vessel. Emma stopped on the dock as Jesse and Becca walked the bridge onto the boat.

"Stayin' here?" Jesse called.

Emma smiled. "Aye! Yer not gettin'me on that deathtrap."

Jesse snapped her a salute. "See ya when we get back, then."

She waved. "Y'better get back here safe."

Jesse gave her a thumbs up and turned to the hectic crew. None of them appeared to notice him while they hurried about so he shrugged and made his way around the boat with Becca at his side.

"You sure about all this?" Becca said.

"No," he said. "But if it's all bullshit, we'll find out soon."

"Just feels like a waste of time."

He nodded. "Could be."

The boat appeared to be stocked up well with not only an array of weapons and harpoons to combat the creature, but survival gear, food and water. But there was something Jesse had never seen before…

He frowned at a large door with LIFE POD printed above it.

"What's a Life Pod?" Jesse said.

A short woman with bright red hair and a dash of freckles across the bridge of her nose stopped long enough to spout, "Tis like a life boat." She frowned at him. "But a pod."

"Oh," Jesse said and chuckled. "Hey, thanks." He held out his hand to shake but she snorted.

"Naw." She held up her hands, which were slimy looking. "Got fish guts all over me. Name's Elsa, though."

"Nice to meet ya," Jesse said. "My name's Jesse and this is Becca."

Elsa frowned and nodded. "Meet'cha." She hurried away without another word.

"Well," Becca said. "She seems nice."

Jesse chuckled and made his way around the lower part of the boat. He found the bait in a large walk-in refrigerator which ranged from chunks of tuna to hog halves. Large drums of chum rested on pallets in the far corner of the refrigerator.

"Damn," Becca said. "This is a serious operation."

"Sure is," Jesse said. He turned to leave the fridge when Becca grabbed his arm. He frowned at her.

"Y'all aren't messing with me, are you?"

Jesse's frown deepened. "What are you talking about?"

"Elle," she said, tears dancing in her eyes. "That thing is named Elle?"

Jesse sighed, forgetting she read the journal. "Yeah. Its name is Elle." He should have expected her to confront him about the name.

She wiped away a few stray tears. She laughed humorlessly. "It's like a sick joke, to be honest."

"I know." He pulled her in for a hug. "I felt the same way when I read it."

She returned his hug, stepped back, and wiped her cheeks. "Sorry. It all just hit me right now. I mean it got me when I was reading, but…"

"I know," Jesse said. "Don't be sorry."

"I didn't mean to get all emotional there." She swiped a stray strand of hair away from her face.

"It's okay," Jesse said and led her out of the refrigerator. "Let's see if this damn thing is real. What do you say?"

She sighed. "Yeah. Not like I got anything better to do."

They walked back up to the deck in time to meet the rest of the crew…and their captain.

14

"Y'must b'Jesse Robins," said a tall man with bright red hair and icy blue eyes. He wore a large, saggy gray turtleneck, scruffy jeans and black rubber boots.

Jesse shook the man's hand, which was strong and covered with heavy calluses. "I am."

The man nodded. "M'name's Lester Campbell." He stepped back a bit and grinned. "Captain Lester Campbell."

"Nice to meet ya, Captain."

This appeared to please Lester. The man nodded and swept an arm at the crew of twelve men and women. The other two must have been inside when they pulled up earlier.

"This is m'crew. Ugly bunch, ain't they?" He chuckled, coughed a bit and pointed at the short woman they met near the walk-in refrigerator. "There's Elsa. She preps all the bait an'helps rig th'lines." He pointed at the man standing next to Elsa. An older bald man with dark bags under his eyes. The guy appeared like he hadn't slept in days. Or hungover. "That'er'mongrel is Ben. He cleans everything." Next to Ben was another man, though much younger, more alert, and with a full head of blond hair. "That'young'un is Buckley. Bloody English bawstard he is. M'first mate."

Buckley laughed, shook his head and patted Lester's shoulder. "Oy, stand down, Captain Campbell."

Lester cackled and walked away and leaned against the door to the wheelhouse of the boat. He winked at Jesse.

"Sorry 'bout that, mate," Buckley said and shook Jesse's hand. "Lester over there loves to pretend he's the captain." He shoved his hands into the pockets of his jeans and smiled. "But I'm really the captain and don't take these goofs too seriously."

Jesse smiled, though wasn't really amused. "Thanks for the heads up."

Buckley cleared his throat. "Anyway. The rest of these folks are here to help you, as am I." He cocked a thumb over his shoulder. "Let's catch a monster, yeah?"

15

"We are going to cruise the loch all night," Buckley said and tapped a map of Loch Ness on the monitor. "Might spend more time in the deepest parts and do some trolling."

Jesse nodded. "Sounds good." He stared at the glowing map for a bit. "Gonna be a long night."

"Yep." Buckley glanced at Elsa. "We'll start chummin' the west coast first."

"Aye," Elsa said and hurried out of the wheelhouse.

"This is a state-of-the-art vessel," Buckley said and tapped another monitor. "If there's anything down there, we'll see it."

Jesse snorted. "You know how many movies I've seen where the captain said the same thing you just did?"

Buckley laughed. "Bloody films ruinin' the real lives of captains everywhere."

"I bet," Jesse said and glanced at Becca. She rolled her eyes. Probably bored. Jesse didn't blame her. Dude talk was rather, more than often, lame. He smiled, shrugged and returned his attention to Buckley. Though he wasn't sure how to respond.

When Jesse looked back again, Becca was gone. He later saw her helping Elsa move pallets of chum with pallet jacks around to the stern. They would be tossing out buckets of chum while the boat trolled about one hundred feet from the west shore.

The old man, Lester, and the rest of the crew appeared to be setting up three harpoon guns. One on either side and one at the bow. Between those, what appeared to be high caliber GPMGs (general purpose machine guns), were mounted on turrets.

"So," Jesse said after the conversation, such as it was, lagged. "What do you think? I mean...*really* think?"

"'Bout what? All this Nessie bollocks?" Buckley chuckled. "Mate, if I wasn't already paid for this lil'scoot around the Loch, I'd be havin' a couple pints at Mickey's'n listenin' to some good music right now."

Jesse blinked. "So, you think the old man was crazy?"

"Edward McComb? Ya damn right. Battier than an old cave in the sticks."

"Why do you think so?"

Buckley steered the boat and gazed out over the dark waters of Loch Ness. The gray light of day was giving way to the somber darkness of dusk.

"Well," Buckley said. "I come from a long line o'sea captains. All the bloody way back to King Henry. An'not a single one told tales of sea monsters. Well, unless y'count whales an'all. Even after the First World War. If there would have been somethin' out there, mate...I'd know."

Jesse nodded. "Fair enough."

"You?"

"Yeah, I don't know." Jesse sighed. "McComb seemed pretty damn convinced."

Buckley smiled, turned the wheel a bit to the right, nodded and looked at Jesse. "'Cos he convinced himself." The man sat in the captain's chair and opened a soda. "Oi, ya ever hear about someone who thinks there's a ghost in a house, even though no one else can see or feel it, or whatever?"

"Sure."

"It's like that. The old man read an old journal and started seein' bloody ghosts, mate." He took a swig from the soda and tipped the bottle at Jesse. "Or giant sea creatures in Loch Ness only nutters *claim* they've seen."

Jesse nodded. "How do you explain the missing people every year?"

Buckley shrugged, drank his soda and capped the bottle. "Serial killer, maybe? Bloody Jack The Ripper's cousin on his mum's side? Who knows."

Once more, Jesse nodded, not sure if he liked Buckley or not. Regardless of not believing there might be a monster in the Loch, the man's vibe was kind of negative. Smarmy, even.

"I'm going to go see how things are going on the deck."

Buckley snorted and waved a hand. "Later, mate."

Jesse left the wheelhouse and stepped out onto the deck. He gave Lester and the crew preparing near the bow a glance and headed to the stern where Becca and Elsa were. The stern also boasted mounted machine guns on either side and what appeared to be another harpoon gun but larger...stouter.

Becca and Elsa dipped gallon pails into the rank chum and tossed the stuff onto the boat's wake. The boat itself chugged along at damn near a snail's pace. The motor didn't make too much noise so shouldn't scare away a large creature like Elle the Loch Ness Monster. The name still unnerved him a bit. Elle...

"Welp," Elsa said. "Y'gonna help'er jus'stand there pissin'?"

Jesse chuckled, grabbed a long rubber glove and a pail. Soon enough, he tossed pailfuls of chum into the dark waters of Loch Ness.

16

They trolled up and down the west side of Loch Ness for about two hours. When nothing happened, Jesse suggested skipping the east side and trolling directly down the middle.

Buckley frowned, then blinked. "Bloody Hell. Why didn't I think 'bout it before?" He tapped a monitor and the map of Loch Ness popped onto the screen. The map glowed in blue, yellow and red wavy lines. At first, Jesse wasn't sure what he was looking at, then...

"The currents," Jesse said.

"Yep," Buckley said. "Should've realized the currents stretch from the center out from the toiling deeper currents." He grunted. "Should've been bloody chummin' the middle."

"Ain't gotta kick'er self, lad," Lester said and chuckled. "Yer not the cap'in anyway."

Buckley snorted and waved a hand at the old man. "Shut it, ya arse. Everything set up on deck?"

"Aye," Lester said. "Good t'go."

Jesse sighed. "Okay." He pointed at the glowing map. Night had already fallen, draping the loch in utter darkness. "Start north and run south."

"But the currents flow north," Buckley said.

"I know." Jesse smirked. "Something I've learned about fishing is you can't really predict every detail." He tapped the monitor. "We start north and troll at eleven or twelve knots. The chum will spread across the Loch. We concentrate all the bait toward the center this way."

Both Buckley and Lester glanced at each other.

"The old man said you're a fisherman," Buckley said and smiled. "Let's catch something, eh?"

Jesse nodded. "Let's go."

Buckley set course for the northern most point of Loch Ness while Jesse, Becca, Elsa and Lester decided to venture below deck to grab something to eat.

"Oi," Buckley called after them. "Bring me a proper English breakfast, Lester!"

Lester snorted and flipped the younger captain off before leaving the wheelhouse.

In the kitchen they made themselves some sandwiches and grabbed some bottled water. In the small dining area, they ate in mostly silence for a few minutes.

Finally, Becca sighed. "Do you all really believe this thing is real? I mean…really?"

Elsa smiled, tore into her sandwich and didn't reply. Lester, on the other hand appeared thoughtful for a moment, then pointed at Becca's bottle of water.

"Do y'believe in that water, lass?"

"Like does it exist or not?"

"Aye, lass. Is it real?"

"Well, yeah."

Lester nodded. "'Cos y'can see it and feel it, aye?"

"Right."

Again, Lester nodded. "Now, d'ya know there are folk on islands that don't know water in bottles exists'n if ya tell'em so they won't believe ya?"

Becca opened her mouth and closed it again.

Lester smiled. "We've seen the creature. Lost friends'n'family cos'o'it." He winked. "We've seen the water in th'bottle."

Becca appeared to think this over a bit, then held up her bottle of water. "If y'all know it's real, then why haven't you done anything about it?"

"Because," Jesse said, "up until now, the local government stopped any and all efforts to kill the thing."

Lester smacked his lips and pointed at Jesse from across the table. Beside him, Elsa upended her water and drank deeply.

"Aye," Lester said. "Can't do much when they got p'trols out durin' this time'o'year."

"Then why did they let this..." Becca gestured around them. "Happen?"

Elsa smacked the table with her hand. "Cos'o'that rich old man." She gave Lester a light shove. "Paid'em off for an entire month too."

"Aye," Lester said and chuckled. "N'matter how rich they are there's always someone richer."

"So, we get a month," Jesse mused.

"Aye." Lester nudged Elsa. "Long'o'nuff for this lass t'go mad."

Elsa rolled her eyes. "Why haven't y'died yet?"

"Cos'ya love me." Lester planted a kiss on the side of Elsa's head.

She shoved him back, both cackling.

Jesse smiled and had a sneaky suspicion they were a couple at one point and now really good friends. Like Becca and him, if he wanted to be honest. He looked at Becca as she finished her sandwich and drank her water. He loved her, yes. But didn't want to open that can of worms again. Or, at least, any time soon. It was probably best they remain close friends. Better that than losing her completely.

A beep sounded followed by Buckley's voice. "Oi, we're approaching the northern point. Where's m'bloody English breakfast?"

Lester chuckled and shook his head. "The lad is funny."

They returned to the deck. Lights from the nearest town glowed not far from the shore. A very low glow, but there. The loch was chilly, nearly silent save for the lapping of the water against the boat and rocks of the beach.

"Y'all got the chumming without me?" Jesse said.

"Aye," Elsa said.

"Where are you going?" Becca said.

"Wheelhouse for a bit," Jesse said. "I want to see what the currents are again."

Becca gave a nod and followed Elsa toward the stern. Lester snapped a salute and met with the rest of the crew at the bow.

In the wheelhouse, Buckley sat in the captain's chair with an open cooler on his lap eating a sandwich.

He nodded at Jesse and swallowed. "I'll steer, you tell me where t'go, mate."

Jesse nodded and surveyed the map of currents. He switched from that map to the depths. At its deepest, the loch was around seven hundred and eighty-eight feet. River Morrison flowed into the loch, which switched the currents around a bit.

"Troll down the middle until River Morrison," Jesse said. "When we arrive at the outlet get as close as you can to it. If we don't, we'll have a large patch without chum."

Buckley cracked open a soda and drank deeply. Finished, he belched and tipped the bottle at Jesse. "Y'know I know Loch Ness well, right?"

Jesse blinked. "No. I didn't know that."

"Ah." Buckley closed the cooler and set it aside. "The ol'man didn't tell yeh then." He stood and glanced at the monitor with the map of Loch Ness. "I've done my fair share of tourist cruises here and know pretty much everything 'bout the loch." He stared at the monitor. The goblin glow of the map gave Buckley's face a green hue.

"Okay?" Jesse stepped back a bit. "Not sure what that has to do with anything."

Buckley smiled and waved a hand. "Oh, nothing. Just wanted t'let you know I *know* Loch Ness."

"Sure. I never said you didn't."

The young captain sighed. "I might've come across a bit harsh, I suppose. But I didn't intend to offend you."

Jesse relaxed a bit. "You didn't offend me. I just didn't see the reason for pointing it out like that."

"Whoa-whoa," Buckley said and held up his hands as if Jesse was pointing a gun at him. "I assure you I was not being a cunt."

Jesse chuckled. "Well, good deal, then." He pointed at the map, which was on the depths still. "I switched this to feet, by the way."

"Bloody Yanks'n'their hatred for the metric system." Buckley clapped Jesse on the shoulder. "Quite alright."

They laughed a bit and worked out a plan.

17

They were about halfway down the length of the loch when a strange sound floated in the air.

"You hear that?" Jesse said, straightening up in his chair.

Buckley stood and squinted out the windshield of the wheelhouse.

The sound, once again, rose and fell.

"Sounds like..." Buckley shook his head.

"Like something dying," Jesse said. He stood and looked out the windshield too.

"Nah," Buckley said. "It's like...a whale, yet none I've ever heard before. Hear that warble?"

Jesse listened. Frowned. "Yeah. Sounds kind of like an ambulance."

"Or..." Buckley cleared his throat. "Someone singing."

"Singing," Jesse mused and listened to the sound before it faded away. "It's weird, though. Sounds like a—"

"Ghost," Buckley interrupted.

Jesse glanced at the man. "Uh, I was gonna say like some kind of opera singer but...sure..."

Buckley grunted. "Y'ever go to a bloody opera, mate?"

"No, but—"

"Operas are fuckin' loud." He pointed to the loch in front of them. "That sound is too soft." He winked at Jesse. "Like a ghost."

Jesse sighed. "Fine. So, what do you think it is?"

"How the hell am I supposed to know?"

Chuckling, Jesse walked to the wheelhouse door. "Thought you're a great sea captain?"

"Bloody hell," Buckley said. "I'm mostly a *charter* captain. I don't—"

A loud thud and the entire boat listed hard to the right. Jesse clung to a railing to stop him from tumbling across the wheelhouse while Buckley hopped into the captain's chair and buckled in.

Buckley shouted, "Hold on!"

"Well, no shit," Jesse shouted back while grappling onto the railing.

The boat dropped back so hard it made Jesse's teeth click together and a weird sensation like his stomach slamming into his chest cavity. Jesse struggled a bit to regain his balance while the boat rocked back and forth.

"Oi!" Buckley said. "Check on my crew!"

Jesse almost told him to fuck off but rushed out of the wheelhouse instead. Not because he was only concerned about the crew, his heart thrummed for Becca. He stumbled onto the deck, skidded into the side railing and regained his balance before falling overboard.

A strong hand grabbed his arm and guided him to the inner railing of the boat.

"Careful, lad," Lester said.

Shaken a bit, Jesse nodded and worked his way toward the stern while the rocking of the boat subsided. When he got to the stern, however, neither Becca nor Elsa was there. A couple of the chum drums lay on their side, spilling foul fish chunks and guts everywhere.

"Becca?" Jesse said and glanced around. There was no sign of her.

He sidestepped the pools of chum and stared out into the darkness of Loch Ness.

"All hands on deck," Buckley announced through the speakers.

Heart thrumming, Jesse turned back in the direction of the bow. "Becca?"

Lester appeared around the corner instead of Becca. "Y'right back'eer, lad?"

Jesse sighed and glanced around. "Yeah, just looking for the ladies who were tossing chum."

Lester frowned. "Haven't seen'em."

A shiver ran through Jesse. "What if that bump…"

Lester shook his head. "I'll get a spotlight out." He patted Jesse's shoulder. "Y'get below deck'n'take a look."

Jesse nodded and ran a hand through his hair. "Yeah. Okay. I'll—"

Water splashed hard against his back, driving him to the deck. He coughed, rolled away from the stern, and scrambled to his feet. He wiped cold water from his face with a trembling hand. There was nothing but darkness beyond the stern. The boat rocked casually back and forth.

"The hell was that?" Lester shouted and moved closer to Jesse.

"I…I don't—"

A massive viper-shaped head slipped out of the darkness. Its eyes glimmered under the pale moonlight and the small lights mounted around the stern. Its semi-long neck, which reminded Jesse of some kind of plesiosaur, curved over the stern. Still, it was weird. The neck wasn't quite long enough.

"Oh," Lester said, voice barely above a whisper. "She's real. She's real, lad."

Jesse opened his mouth and closed it again. He couldn't talk. Couldn't move.

The creature nudged one of the chum drums with its scaly snout, nostrils flaring. A deep growl rumbled the cool, damp air. It sniffed the drums. Lester, meanwhile, inched his way toward the bow. No matter how much

Jesse shook his head, the old man continued. It took all of Jesse's strength not to shout, "Don't move, you old fool!" He held it back. Barely.

So far, though, the creature didn't seem to notice Jesse or Lester. It nudged the drums of chum and licked at the pools accumulating on the deck. Maybe Lester had the right idea, then. But when Jesse tried to move, his legs didn't work right and, with the slight rocking of the boat, stumbled a bit. His boots thumped the deck.

He glanced at the creature, but it wasn't at the stern anymore. Like it simply vanished out of thin air.

"C'mon," Lester whispered. His eyes were wide, bottom lip trembling. "Make a run for it now."

Jesse spared a quick glance around and nodded. "Go."

They broke into a sprint for the walkway leading to the wheelhouse and bow. Lester stumbled a bit, slamming a shoulder into the side of the cabin. Jesse caught the old man before he fell and then Lester bolted again. He ran fast for an old man. Jesse followed, not able to keep his balance quite as well because of the slight rocking of the boat. What was it sailors said? Haven't got your sea legs yet? Something like that.

He swayed, bumping into the cabin here and there and avoiding the railing as much as possible.

Lester was just about to the bow when water exploded over the side of the boat and crashed into him. The old man slipped and dropped to his knees. He was just getting to his feet when the large reptilian head darted out of the darkness. Its massive jaws snapped down over the top half of the man. Blood sprayed, painting the door to the wheelhouse red.

Jesse skidded to a stop, heart hammering. For a moment, time seemed to slip into slow motion. Lester's right hand twitched. Someone screamed, but it felt distant. Dream-like. Then it was as if the Universe slapped the world across the face and everything sped up.

The monster yanked Lester off the boat and disappeared into the dark waters of Loch Ness.

Jesse gaped at the blood-splattered wheelhouse door for a while, he wasn't sure how long, before Buckley opened the door and stepped onto the walkway.

"Uh," Buckley said and glanced around. "What…" Then he saw all the blood, especially the small pool he stood in. He gasped and looked at Jesse. "What in the bloody *Hell*?" He blinked. "Literally."

Jesse shoved the man away from the side of the boat toward the bow. "It killed Lester."

Stumbling, Buckley said, "Lester? What—"

"The Loch Ness monster killed Lester," Jesse said. "We need people on those guns."

"Guns?" Buckley said. "I thought we were supposed to try catching it alive first…"

Jesse blinked. "What? No, we're—"

"You have your financier," a woman said behind him. "And so do we."

Jesse turned around to find Elsa pointing a gun at him.

"What the fuck?" Jesse glanced around until his gaze fell on Buckley. "What is this?"

Buckley sighed. "Elsa…put that away." Gone was his English accent, replaced with a light Russian one.

Elsa rolled her eyes and holstered the gun.

"Jesse," Buckley said. "We must capture the beast alive and ship it to our employer or we'll be killed."

Jesse shook his head and glared at Elsa. "Where's Becca?"

Elsa smiled. "She's below deck taking a nap."

Anger flashed through Jesse. "What did you do to her?"

Elsa's smile never faltered. "Just gave her a little something to take the edge off."

He darted forward, snatched the pistol from its holster and moved away from Buckley and the crew. He pointed the gun at each of the crew, falling on Buckley last.

"Becca and I are taking the lifeboat and leaving."

Buckley shook his head. "I can't let that happen." He sighed. "Nothing personal, right? We just—"

Something struck the left side of the boat hard enough to toss everyone off their feet. Jesse slid across the deck and grabbed a railing attached to the wheelhouse. If not for the railing, he would have slammed into the side of the boat with about half of the crew.

Half of the boat lifted off the water, nearly capsized, then crashed back down. Water splashed onto the deck, drenching Jesse and the crew. The boat rocked heavily back and forth. Someone screamed. Someone else shouted something in what might have been Russian.

While the boat began to settle, Jesse took the moment to slip away and go below deck. He didn't have a plan, except for finding Becca, securing the lifeboat, and getting the hell away from Loch Ness. He didn't think Mr. Toole set him up, but Jesse wasn't exactly confident either.

Russia was trying to reclaim the thing they lost decades ago, and Jesse didn't want any part of it. He didn't even care about the money anymore. Hell, he was regretting even coming to Scotland in the first place.

He found Becca on a cot in a small room not far from the kitchen. He shook her. "Hey." But she didn't move, let alone wake up. He spotted a tiny puncture mark surrounded by a small bruise on the side of her neck. She'd been drugged, he knew that...but with what? There wasn't a syringe or anything else in the room. Not even a trashcan.

She was breathing, though, which eased his nerves a bit.

"No, no, Jesse."

Buckley stood just outside the doorway pointing a sawed-off shotgun at Jesse. Water dripped from the tip of his nose and soggy clothes, creating a small pool around his boots.

"We're getting off this boat," Jesse said, hand gripping Elsa's pistol. "I didn't sign up to be a Russian pawn."

Buckley snorted. "What makes you think it will let you paddle to the shore?"

Jesse sighed. The man had a point and it crossed Jesse's mind more than once, but…

"We'll take our chances."

"That is stupidity, my friend." Buckley lowered the shotgun. His face softened. "Listen, my crew…me…we are not the bad guys."

"Right," Jesse said. "You just work for the bad guys."

"Not work for…forced to comply."

Jesse blinked. "Forced? I thought Elsa said y'all are getting paid."

Buckley cleared his throat and glanced over his shoulder to make sure no one was behind him. He returned his attention to Jesse. "I'm a cod fisherman by trade. One of the best and our Oligarchs took notice." He lowered his gaze a bit. "They have my children, Jesse."

"Took notice?" Jesse frowned. "So, you are getting paid?"

"No," Buckley said. "They want the creature. The one Dr. Pavel Gusev stole, and they lost. My payment is getting my children back safe and sound."

Jesse nodded. "Understood." He thought about it for a second or two. "So, why now? They had all of this time to search for the thing. Why now?"

"Oh," Buckley waved a dismissive hand. "That's easy. McComb."

"McComb? How—"

"They've been monitoring this region for a long time, Jesse, and intercepted communications between McComb and someone else, confirming the creature's existence in Loch Ness."

"Someone else," Jesse mused, thinking about his mother.

"Yes." Buckley ran a hand through his wet hair and sighed. "I need your help, Jesse." He looked Jesse directly in the eyes. "Please. To save my children."

Jesse glanced at Becca then looked at Buckley. "Let's bag us the Loch Ness Monster."

Buckley smiled and stepped aside. "Thank you."

18

He made sure Becca was covered up and pillows layered around the floor of the room just in case the creature tried to capsize the boat again. Hopefully they would bag the monster before that happened again, though. Or, ideally, she woke up and was able to protect herself better.

Jesse shut the door and returned to the deck.

It was almost one o'clock in the morning.

"So," he said to Buckley and the crew. "It likes the chum. I think that's why it attacked. It wants more."

One of the crew members, a stout man maybe in his mid-forties, raised his meaty hand.

"Yeah?"

The man cleared his throat and spoke in a Russian accent so thick it was difficult for Jesse to understand.

"We go home now." At least that was the gist Jesse got from the man.

Jesse nodded. "You'll go home when we catch the monster. No exceptions." He looked at Buckley. "We continue chumming as planned, but I want people manning the guns and nets."

Buckley gave a solid nod. "Agreed." To the crew, he said, "Jesse is your superior on the deck. Obey his orders."

The crew all looked at Jesse. It was like being a sergeant in the Army again. All eyes on him. And it was interesting, after all those years, how he slipped right back into the role.

"Elsa and...you," he said and pointed at a lanky man next to her. "You toss the chum."

Elsa glanced at Buckley, obviously for approval. He nodded and she sighed. Elsa nudged the man next to her and they hurried toward the stern.

Jesse turned to Buckley. "Keep a steady course south. Don't troll, though. I don't want this thing getting close enough to capsize us." He cocked a thumb over his shoulder at the crew. "It will also give them time enough to aim the harpoons and nets."

Buckley nodded. "Yes." He started toward the wheelhouse, but Jesse grabbed the man's arm.

"Do you have motion sensors on this boat?"

Buckley blinked. "Yes."

Jesse nodded. "Okay, let's go check it out." He glanced at the crew. "One of you man the net at the stern."

He followed Buckley to the wheelhouse. Buckley tapped the monitor next to the one with the depth and current maps.

"Okay," Buckley said and tapped an icon that looked like a video camera with a blue circle around it. An outline of the boat appeared at the center of the screen, green lines spread out around it. Every now and then a tiny spot blipped on the screen. "If anything comes within one fifty meters we'll see it."

Jesse snorted. "We should've had this thing fired up earlier."

"Yes," Buckley said and chuckled a bit. His Russian accent was so light, he almost spoke perfect English. "We should have and do now."

"I'll keep an eye on these monitors," Jesse said. "Just keep us at a steady clip. Maybe a couple miles per hour—"

"Knots," Buckley said. "We go by knots."

Jesse opened his mouth and shut it again. He was about to speak when Buckley said, "Ten knots is about ten miles an hour or a bit more."

Jesse clenched his jaw and glanced at the motion sensor screen. "Let's try twenty knots, then."

"Only ten above what I was trolling?"

"Yeah. To start. Let's see what happens."

"You think it wants to hunt, don't you?"

Jesse nodded. "Yeah. It's an apex predator like a northern pike or shark. It wants to catch its food."

"Sure," Buckley said and sat in the captain's chair. He started the engine and looked at Jesse. "Fingers crossed."

"Yeah." Jesse turned to the monitors. "Fingers crossed."

19

About half an hour or so crawled by and no sign of Elle II. No sign of a monster. No signs of life out there, period. Absolutely nothing blipped on the motion detection screen. As if Loch Ness itself was nothing more than a large, empty, dark gash. Void of life.

They were already floating toward the southernmost point of the loch.

"You want to know what I believe?" Buckley said as he shut the engine down and looked at Jesse. "I believe there are tunnels going from one loch to another and to the ocean itself."

Jesse nodded and returned his attention to the monitors. "Why do you think that?"

"Well, let me ask you this…" He sat up a bit. "How does this thing get around? And surely there isn't enough food in this loch to sustain it, right? We know there is a tunnel to the ocean, but what about the other lochs?"

"I mean, sure," Jesse said. "You think this is where it breeds or—"

"No. I believe it comes here to rest before making a long swim across the ocean."

Jesse glanced at Buckley. He thought about McComb's journal and how he thought the creature came to Loch Ness to breed or to simply eat.

"Where do you think it goes?"

Buckley shrugged. "From what I have heard…the Americas. Australia is another one I have heard."

"Yeah, McComb mentioned it travelling in his journal. His theory…that it has given birth to a couple more like it. Just as he theorized this one is not the original creature Pavel was trying to protect."

"Right." Buckley nodded. "Right." He appeared to think about it for a few seconds. "That makes sense. That there are more out there."

"Yeah, I—"

A small beep snapped Jesse's attention back to the monitor. A large red mass slipped swiftly across the monitor toward the boat. "Oh, shit, it's—"

The entire boat quaked though didn't lift enough to worry Jesse about capsizing. He stumbled, grabbed the speaker mic and thumbed the side button.

"Everyone! Get the nets and guns ready!"

"Not the guns!" Buckley shouted.

Jesse shot the man a glare. "Calm down. It's a precaution."

Buckley shot out of his chair and drew his pistol. He pointed it at Jesse. "No guns!"

"Put it away," Jesse said and stepped forward. Buckley's hand holding the pistol trembled. It told Jesse all he needed to know. "We will save your kids."

Eventually, Buckley holstered the gun, sighed, and ran a hand through his blond hair. "S-Sorry."

Jesse moved closer and glowered at the man. "You pull a gun on me again, and I'll shoot you myself."

Buckley blinked at Jesse.

"Get in the chair and drive this thing." Jesse thought about taking Buckley's pistol then decided against it. "If we net this thing...all hell will break loose, and we'll need you to run the boat to avoid being capsized until the tranquilizers take hold."

Buckley blinked again...frowned. "Where are you going?"

"To make sure the crew is safe and bag this thing."

After a few seconds or so, Buckley nodded. He slipped into the captain's chair without another word.

Jesse gave the motion monitor another glance. The large red blob was near the stern.

"It's going after the chum barrels again," he said and hurried out of the wheelhouse.

The damp chill of the air struck him like a slap across the face. He slid on the blood-slicked deck outside of the wheelhouse door. Lester's blood. The crew hadn't bothered to clean it up. Jesse rushed to the stern where Elsa and the other guy, whose name Jesse's brain spaced on, were still tossing chum.

"Each of you get on a gun," Jesse shouted as he mounted the net canon. "Stay alert. If I miss and it attacks...shoot it."

"But we're not supposed to kill it," Elsa said.

"I know," Jesse said. "I'm going to try and catch it first. Do you have a tranquilizer gun?"

"Yes," Elsa said and ran back toward the cabin.

Jesse glanced at the man. "Be ready. If I miss and it attacks, shoot it."

The man didn't appear to understand at first, then nodded. He got the machine gun ready.

Jesse fixed his attention on the water. He watched it rise and fall under the moonlight. The night fell silent. The only sounds were of the water lapping against the boat and the man arming one of the machine guns clearing his throat. Jesse imagined the creature creeping just under the surface watching him. Measuring him up. Hell, maybe it was.

"Got the tranq gun," Elsa said behind him.

"Good." Jesse adjusted his stance a bit and pointed the net cannon at the water. "Once I net it, I want you to put three tranquilizers into it."

"I could shoot it with a tranq when I first see it," Elsa said.

"No." Jesse glanced over his shoulder at her. "Wait until I net it. If you put it to sleep in the water it could drown."

She nodded and stood near the net cannon; tranquilizer gun ready to rock.

He waited awhile, not sure how long, maybe fifteen minutes or so. When the monster didn't show itself, he secured the net cannon and ran to the wheelhouse.

"What are you doing?" Buckley said as Jesse rushed in. "It hasn't moved. I've been watching."

Jesse frowned, glanced at the monitor, saw the large red blob at the stern and looked at Buckley.

"You have walkie-talkies?"

Buckley cocked his head to the side. "Walkie…what?"

"Radios." Jesse mimed using a walkie-talkie.

"Oh," Buckley said and jumped out of his chair. "Yes. Right…" He rummaged around in a drawer and brought out a pair of black walkie-talkies. "Here."

"Do they work?"

Buckley turned them both on and a loud screech filled the wheelhouse. He quickly shut them off and smiled at Jesse. "Sounds like they do."

Jesse snorted. "Yeah. No kidding." He took one of them. "I'll be on channel one."

Buckley turned the top knob of his to one.

"Okay," Jesse said. "Let me know if it moves. No matter what. Keep me fully updated."

"I will," Buckley said.

Jesse gave the man a nod and left the wheelhouse with the radio in hand. The creature was still hanging out at the stern, so—

It burst out of the water, jumping partially onto the stern of the boat. Elsa screamed and backpedaled, avoiding the monster's snapping maw. It roared, hissed and lunged for Elsa again. She shot a tranquilizer dart into its shoulder, slipped on a slick of chum on the deck and dropped the tranquilizer gun.

Jesse slid through the chum, grabbed Elsa and shoved her away before the creature tore into her. He stumbled away, narrowly avoiding those massive jaws, and picked up the tranquilizer gun. The creature shifted and the boat listed severely to the right. Jesse grabbed the hand railing, stopping himself from tumbling into the water.

The monster chortled, as if laughing at Jesse. Maybe it was.

"Son of a bitch," Jesse said and aimed the tranq gun at the creature.

Its yellow eyes fixed on Jesse and for a moment, he thought he saw some kind of intelligence. Like it knew what it was doing and had a plan.

"Goodnight." Jesse's finger began to squeeze the trigger.

A millisecond before he could squeeze the trigger all the way, the creature shifted its weight again, jolting Jesse into the cabin. He lost his grip on the tranq gun and it fell to the deck, sliding directly in front of Elle II. The actual Loch Ness Monster. It glanced at the gun, then appeared to smirk.

The lanky man on the machine gun on the left side of the stern dismounted the thing and opened fire at the monster. Spraying bullets everywhere. Jesse ducked behind the cabin, hoping one of those stray bullets didn't crash through the walls of the cabin and hit him.

The creature shrieked.

When Jesse, thanking whatever gods there were out there that he was still alive, peeked around the corner, the lanky man was on his knees trying to lift the machine gun. How the guy was able to heft the damn thing to begin with was nothing short of amazing. Those guns were heavy. Adrenaline could be one hell of a strength enhancer, though. Jesse knew that much from experience.

The creature, though...it was inching its way closer to him. Jesse wasn't sure if it was blood or more chum sloshing on the deck. He couldn't tell if the monster was hurt or not.

The lanky man's strength, however, appeared to be waning. He tried lifting the machine gun to fire at the creature again but couldn't. His teeth gritted. The veins in his neck bulged. Try as he might, though, the adrenaline rush had ended, leaving him vulnerable.

Jesse glanced at the machine gun near him, thought about using it like the lanky man did, then decided to go for the tranq gun. Which was extremely close to the monster, but...

The creature sprang forward and chomped the lanky man's left arm off. Blood spurted onto the deck, mixing with the water and chum. The man, eyes wide, stared at the spurting stump where his arm used to be. Shock. Jesse had personally seen it far too many times in the past.

"Hey," Jesse shouted, drawing the monster's attention. He drew the pistol he had taken from Elsa and aimed it at one of the creature's eyes.

He was about to squeeze the trigger when the lanky man unleashed one of the loudest screams Jesse had ever heard. The monster whipped its attention back to the man.

"Shit," Jesse said. He thought about pumping a couple of rounds into the thing's neck but decided against it. If the tranq wasn't working, then the creature's hide might be too thick. Even if the pistol was a forty-five, he didn't think it would penetrate deep enough to do any harm.

The lanky man continued to scream and no matter how much Jesse tried to get the monster's attention the wailing and screaming drowned out his voice.

From around the far corner, Elsa stopped. Her gaze slipped over the lanky man and all the blood to the monster half on and half off the boat. Surprisingly the boat hadn't shown any signs of sinking.

The creature's attention shifted from the lanky man to Elsa. She held a trembling hand to her mouth, eyes wide.

"Get away from there," Jesse shouted, though Elsa didn't seem to hear him over lanky man's screaming.

"What the hell is—" Buckley said behind Jesse as he walked by the cabin. "Holy *shit*."

"Get back to the wheelhouse," Jesse roared.

Buckley blinked. Then it seemed to dawn on him. He stumbled, spun around and ran back toward the wheelhouse.

Jesse sighed, shook his head and motioned at Elsa, hoping to gain her attention. No luck, though. She was too rapt by the creature. A thing that should not be.

"Fuck it," Jesse said. He lifted the pistol, aimed it at the monster's neck, and squeezed the trigger.

The Loch Ness Monster shrieked and snapped its head in Jesse's direction. Its yellow eyes gleamed with rage. A deep growl bubbled in its throat.

Jesse aimed the pistol again and put a round in its eye.

Its shriek blasted through the lanky man's screams and shook Jesse's chest. The monster lunged at Jesse. He jumped away just in time to not get chomped in half. It bit onto the railing, hissed, and crawled a bit more onto the boat. Its weight tilted the vessel. Any more and it would sink the boat.

Buckley stepped out of the wheelhouse and Jesse waved a hand at him. "Punch the gas to the floor!"

But Buckley didn't move. He held on to the door while the boat continued to tilt upward. His attention wasn't on the boat, nor Jesse, but the monster inching its way closer to Jesse.

Jesse gripped the railing on the cabin and waved at Buckley again. "Drive!"

He wasn't sure of the proper words to use, but Buckley appeared to understand this time. He slipped back into the wheelhouse.

Jesse glanced over his shoulder just as the monster shrieked at him. It snapped its large jaws, pointy teeth clicking. It continued trying to climb onto the boat to kill Jesse. Or was that its only purpose? What if it knew it could sink the boat with its weight? Could it really be that intelligent?

A loud revving noise cut through Jesse's frantic thoughts. His grip tightened on the cabin's railing. The creature stopped shrieking and looked around. It was then Jesse noticed, with the help of the boat's outside lights, he missed the eye. Instead, the bullet entered near the inside corner of the eye. Maybe it shattered the creature's nasal cavity a bit? If so, Jesse couldn't tell.

Elle II, the Loch Ness Monster, flopped backward as if trying to get off the boat.

Then the entire boat jolted forward. The creature shrieked and rolled off the boat into the loch. The boat crashed down. Water sprayed in every direction, drenching Jesse. Once the bobbing and swaying of the boat subsided, Jesse vomited from motion sickness and made his way back to check on the lanky man and Elsa.

The man was laid on his back, Elsa kneeling at his side.

Jesse kneeled next to Elsa.

"He lost too much blood," she said, her voice so low he barely heard it.

The lanky man's face was nearly gray, lips blue. His head lolled back and forth.

Jesse quickly tied his belt above the shredded stump without much hope. "Help me move him into the cabin."

Elsa sniffled and shook his head. "He's dead." She wiped tears from her cheeks, stood and walked away.

Jesse frowned and checked the man's pulse. After a bit, he sighed and bowed his head. "Damn."

He carried the man into the cabin anyway and covered him with a spare sheet.

"W-What's going on?" Becca said behind him. "Was I drugged? Did that bitch drug me?"

Jesse turned. "Yep. Elsa drugged you. But listen we—"

"Where is she?" Becca said and glanced around. Her hands curled into fists.

"Wait—"

"I am right here," Elsa said and stepped out of the shadows.

Becca spun around, fists trembling at her sides. "How *dare* you fucking drug me."

"Becca, hold on…"

"Shut up," Becca said and shot a glare over her shoulder at him.

"I had to," Elsa said.

"What do you…wait…" She turned a bit to look at Jesse. "Why does she sound Russian now?"

"Because she is," Jesse said. "So is the rest of the crew."

"Not Lester," Elsa said. "He was Scottish."

Becca frowned. "What…? I don't—"

"They're a Russian crew sent by their government to capture the creature alive," Jesse said. "Not by choice, either."

"What do you mean 'not by ch—"

A loud thud quaked the boat. A glass fell off a nearby counter and shattered on the floor.

Becca glanced at Jesse. "What was that?"

Jesse checked the pistol's mag and slapped it back home. "The Loch Ness Monster."

20

"What are we going to do?" Becca said behind Jesse as he hurried toward the wheelhouse.

"I don't know," he said and opened the wheelhouse door. He looked at her. "Stay close to Elsa and the crew. Get behind one of the machine guns if you can."

She snorted. "Machine guns? Me?"

"Yeah. Have Elsa or someone show you how to use one before it attacks again."

Her eyes widened. "*Again?*"

Jesse nodded. "I'll be back on the deck soon. Get with Elsa and see if she'll train you on something. I need to talk to the captain about a new plan."

"Sure. It's not like I've been drugged for the last couple of hours or anything and he wants me to shoot a goddamn machine gun." Becca chuckled, waved a dismissive hand at him and walked away.

He didn't want to leave her in the hands of Russian monster hunters for hire, but he needed to form a better plan with Buckley.

The man himself sat in the captain's chair.

"We need to come up with a—"

"Plan?" Buckley said. He stared out the window in front of him.

Jesse blinked. "Uh…yeah." There was something off about Buckley again. "So, we should—"

"You are going to get my children killed."

Jesse frowned, stunned. He opened his mouth and closed it again.

Buckley swiveled around in the chair to look at Jesse. "I heard gunshots."

"Those gunshots saved my life."

"Elsa told me you got Brock killed with your recklessness."

"What?" Jesse shook his head. "No. Brock saved me."

Buckley glared at Jesse. "Who shot the creature?"

"He did," Jesse said. "Then I did to save Elsa." He glared right back at Buckley. "Look, we'll capture it if we can, but that plan isn't working out so well. You lost two of your crew members already." He glanced at the motion monitor. A large red blob floated slowly around the boat. "We need a new plan."

"Like what?"

Jesse shook his head. "I'm not sure. That's why I'm here. So, we can put our heads together and figure something out." He tapped the monitor. "Hopefully before she attacks again."

Buckley sighed and nodded. "Okay. What are your thoughts?"

"I think we should make it chase us," Jesse said. "Wear it out to the point where we can net it and tranquilize it."

"I can do that," Buckley said. "Run it for an hour?"

"Start at twenty minutes." Jesse gestured at the motion monitor. "I don't want it to lose interest if it can't catch us."

"Okay. Slow troll?"

Jesse shook his head. "Let's go a couple knots faster than we were." He snapped his fingers as a new thought sprang into his mind. "We give chase and then drift for a couple of minutes. Trigger a hunting response instead of a mindless attack."

Buckley nodded slowly. "And what if it does attack while we're drifting?"

"Oh," Jesse said. "If this plan works I'm planning on it taking the bait."

"Taking the bait," Buckley mused.

"Troll for an hour with drifts every ten minutes." Jesse nodded at the bow. "I'll have half of the crew there and take the rest to the stern with me."

Buckley sighed. "Just please do not kill it."

Jesse patted the man's shoulder. "I'll do my best not to."

Buckley nodded and looked away. "I'm worried about my children."

"I know," Jesse said. "I promised we'll get them back and I make it a hard point to keep my promises."

After a few seconds, Buckley nodded and plopped down in his chair. "We will see, then."

"Yep," Jesse said and walked toward the wheelhouse door. "I'm going to send Becca in to watch the motion monitor. I want you both to communicate and synchronize accordingly. And communicate with us so we're prepared."

Buckley managed a weak smile. "We will."

"Good." Jesse stepped out of the wheelhouse and gathered the crew to announce the new plan.

21

The original crew lost two members, but with Jesse and Becca they were back to being a strong ten-person crew again.

Well, at least competent, anyway. Both Jesse and Becca needed to learn a few things about boat safety and what would happen when Buckley slowed to a drift. All this training was done within an hour. About ten minutes before the first drift, Becca entered the wheelhouse. Jesse hurried to the stern where Elsa and three other people chucked chum overboard.

This time, Jesse didn't even need the motion monitor to know where the creature was. Every few seconds, with the help of the moonlight, he caught the creature's serpentine head pop out of the water. Good. The plan was working so far.

"Prepare to drift," he announced. "The creature will come at us fast, so you'll need to be quick."

"We tranq it then net it?" Elsa said.

"No," Jesse said. "Net it then tranq."

She gave a firm nod and got behind the net cannon. The two men were on the machine guns, while a third man waited with the tranquilizer gun. Jesse stood close to the guy with the gun and watched the creature feed on the chum.

The boat's motor slowed a bit then cut off completely, sending them into a drift. Jesse lurched forward a bit to keep his balance as did the man with the tranq gun. Waves sloshed against the stern, pushing the boat forward.

Jesse frowned at the moonlit loch, but the monster didn't surface. He moved forward a few steps and stopped. The entire boat fell into absolute silence.

Jesse's heart thrummed. The creature was intelligent...unpredictable. He kept forgetting and reminded himself now. It's not a damn northern pike that could be baited so easily. Hell, they got lucky with the chum. It also surprised him that it was following them.

Eventually, the drifting slowed to the point of barely moving. A near stop. If not for the small waves of the loch, the boat wouldn't be moving at all.

"It's gone," Becca said through the boat speakers. "It was right there but now it's gone."

"Shit," Jesse said and moved closer to the stern's rail. He watched the moonlit water for a moment then glanced at Elsa. "Keep an eye on things. I'll be right back."

Elsa nodded.

Jesse ran to the wheelhouse. Becca stood in front of the motion monitor while Buckley sat in his chair. He gave Jesse a shrug.

"It was right there," Becca said and pointed at a space just off the stern. "Looked like it was about to ram right into the boat. Then it just...disappeared."

Jesse stared at the monitor. "Where are you...?"

"Should I continue?" Buckley said.

"Yeah," Jesse said after a bit. "Same speed and everything. Let's see if it pops up." He gave Becca a weak smile and left the wheelhouse.

"Anything?" Jesse asked.

Elsa straightened. "No. Nothing."

"Okay, we're going to try it again."

She rolled her eyes. "The captain should go ashore and forget all of this. This is not worth the money."

Jesse almost asked her about Buckley's kids when the creature burst out of the water, mouth gaping. It clamped onto the arm of the man behind the left-side machine gun. The man screamed as the monster lifted him off his feet. Blood rained onto the deck. Jesse drew the pistol he had taken from Elsa earlier, aimed, and put a bullet between the creature's eyes.

The monster reared and shrieked, releasing the man. The man crashed to the deck sobbing and staring at his ruined arm. Still shrieking, the creature backed away from the boat and into the moonlight. It shook its head and splashed water in every direction. Elsa and the other two men pulled their injured crew member away from the railing and closer to the cabin. They began to tie on a makeshift tourniquet to his chewed-up arm.

Jesse got behind the machine gun and was ready to obliterate the thrashing thing when his attention was drawn to the tranquilizer gun about to fall overboard. He swept the gun up and aimed it at the creature's throat. It snapped its gaze at Jesse, appeared to, even in its pain, notice the gun and dove into the water. Waves sloshed heavily against the boat, rocking it.

"It's gone," Becca said through the speakers.

He stepped away from the side of the boat, heart bashing itself against his ribs. He got his breathing under control and hurried to help the man with the mutilated arm. Most of the skin had been stripped off and it appeared to be broken in several places. One of the bones in the man's forearm poked through the skin like a broken scarlet stick. Someone had tied a strip of blue cloth just above the man's bicep, which stemmed the blood flow.

"Let's get him below deck," Jesse said. "We'll get him—"

"Jesse! It's—"

Becca was in mid-sentence when the monster shot out of the water and latched onto Elsa. She managed a tiny scream before it yanked her off the boat and into the dark waters of Loch Ness. Jesse and the other two men gaped at the empty space where Elsa had stood. Water lapped against the boat.

"Jesse?" Becca shouted through the speakers. "Everything okay back there?"

Jesse opened his mouth to tell her and shut it again. He unclipped the radio from the waistband of his jeans and pressed the mic button and said, "I'm okay. One injured and…" He paused. "We lost Elsa." He released the button and sighed.

One of the men shuffled away. The other trembled; a large wet patch spread through the crotch and down the legs of his jeans. The man with the mutilated arm groaned and writhed on the deck.

Jesse pressed the mic button again. "Gonna need some help back here."

22

"I have lost four of my crew," Buckley said and shook his head. He frowned at Jesse. "None of your plans have worked."

Jesse backhanded a coffee mug off a table in the wheelhouse, shot forward and grabbed Buckley by the collar of his shirt. He yanked the man closer.

"Listen, you motherfucker. I'm trying to save your kids, but this thing is a lot smarter than we thought."

He shoved Buckley away and pointed at the boat's wheel. "You're fuckin' lucky I don't have you take us back to shore right now. Because I've thought about it dozens of times now."

"We should go anyway," Becca said. "I really don't wanna die out here."

Jesse nodded. "Me either." He gave Buckley a withering look. "Do you have proof that the oligarchs are holding your kids hostage?"

"What?" one of the crew who had taken over Elsa's place in command said. A wiry man, maybe in his late thirties, with messy dark hair. Jesse thought his name might be Uri or something like that. His Russian accent was so thick it was difficult to understand him. "You never told us about your children."

Buckley threw up his arms in exasperation. "Fine. I don't have kids and the oligarchs are payin' me to wrangle the creature." And all at once, he sounded like he was from Texas. No wonder his accents were so light.

Jesse pointed his pistol at the man. "Who are you? Because you're sure as shit not a Russian sailor."

The blond man snorted, nodded and sat in the captain's chair. He brought out a bottle of Jack Daniels from a bottom cabinet, screwed the top off, and took a deep pull from the bottle. He hissed and shook his head.

"I kind of monster hunter, dude," Buckley said. "People pay me to wrangle all kinds of creatures." He tipped the bottle at Jesse and smiled. "Like y'all getting paid to kill the thing."

Jesse lowered the pistol. "If you're a pro then why can't you catch this thing?"

"We have been misled," the Russian man, Uri, said. He spat in Buckley's direction. "Elsa, John, and Lester are dead because of you."

Buckley took a swig from his whiskey bottle, burped and nodded. "Yup. Didn't want'em to die, though." He capped the bottle, slipped it back into the cabinet and stood. "And no more will die tonight."

Everyone in the wheelhouse fell silent for a bit.

"Here's the new plan," Buckley said. He looked at Jesse. "We kill it."

Jesse smiled. "About damn time." He pointed at Buckley. "But if you fuck around...you won't have to worry about the Loch Ness Monster eating you. Understand?"

Buckley gave a single, firm nod. "Yup."

"Good," Jesse said. "So, it's shoot to kill now. We'll troll just like before with the chum but I want everyone on a gun. The moment it pops its head up...open fire." He glanced at all three people in the wheelhouse. "Understand?"

Buckley chuckled. "I'm just drivin' the boat, man."

"And you better do it well." Jesse pointed at Becca. "When she says it's closing in, drift. When I radio to move, move."

Buckley nodded. "Yup." He turned the wheel and appeared to drift into deep thought while staring out the windshield.

Jesse gave Becca a pat on the shoulder. "You got this. Same thing you did before."

She smiled, though there didn't seem to be any confidence behind it. To the man, Uri or whatever, Jesse said, "Let's get the rest of the crew ready."

Uri nodded and rushed out of the wheelhouse before Jesse could move.

Jesse gave Becca and Buckley a final look and followed Uri onto the deck. They got people behind the machine guns and Uri showed Jesse the small armory below deck while Buckley gradually increased the boat's speed.

"What's that thing?" Jesse pointed at what appeared to be a robot.

"Oh. Russian prototype diving suit, I think. Buckley knows more about it."

Jesse nodded, took an AK-47 and a couple of mags. He handed Uri the other AK and an extra mag. Jesse replaced the mag for the pistol and closed the doors.

"Okay, let's kill this thing." He smiled. "Maybe we'll be done and ready to share a pint at one of those pubs on the main drag."

Uri snorted. "Only if they got vodka."

Jesse chuckled and led the way back up to the deck.

On deck, a slight breeze had picked up. A cold one. The crew already slipped into their jackets and caps. Jesse started to go below deck again to find at least a jacket to quell the chill—

"It's behind us," Becca said through the speakers. "Closing in fast."

Without Jesse saying a word, the team got behind the machine guns. Well, at least at the bow. The stern...

Steeling himself, he ran toward the stern and the boat decreased its speed.

Jesse managed a gasp and slammed into the outer railing. If the AK-47 hadn't been strapped to him, it would have gone flying out into Loch Ness. Hell, *he* almost went flying into Loch Ness. He caught himself, just barely, on the rail and flung himself backward to the cabin. Jesse leaned against the cabin until he gained his balance and hurried to the stern.

Uri was behind the machine gun turret on the left, another guy manned the gun on the right. A woman continued to toss chum overboard. Jesse motioned for her to step away from the stern. She did and Jesse readied his AK-47. He watched the moonlit waters. With a pistol clutched in her hands—the woman he motioned away—stepped on the other side of the net cannon. He grunted, smiled and focused on the water.

They waited for what felt like hours but was probably only about five minutes.

Jesse radioed the wheelhouse. "Anything?"

After a couple of seconds, Buckley said, "It's right there, man. About five feet from the stern, Becca says."

Jesse frowned at the wavy water glistening under the moonlight. He watched a severed fish head bob for a few seconds before slipping under the surface. Elle II was sucking the chum from the surface while trying not to let everyone know it was there. Trying to be sneaky.

What confused Jesse, though, was if it knew the boat meant it harm, why would it keep following? Unless...

"It's moving," Becca said through the speakers. "Looks like it's going under the—"

The entire boat rose and fell so hard and fast Jesse's stomach jumped to his chest. He vomited from the motion and grabbed onto the cabin's railing. One of the men, not Uri, ran for the cabin door and the boat rose and fell again. This time much higher. The jolt sent the man flying. He landed near the outer railing, managed a cry of pain, and the boat rose and fell hard, flinging him off the deck and into the water.

He only screamed once then…silence.

For the moment, the boat remained on the water and Jesse scrambled to help Uri and the woman up. He wasn't sure where the other man was. Maybe he got flung off the boat too. Together, they made their way around the cabin to the bow.

"Tell them to shoot anything that moves," Jesse told Uri.

Uri nodded and ran to talk to the people manning the guns. Jesse made sure the woman was okay and entered the wheelhouse.

"It's still under us," Becca said the moment he stepped through the door. "Hasn't moved for at least five minutes."

Jesse pointed at Buckley. "Move. Go as fast as you can as soon as you can and don't let up until I tell you."

Buckley frowned. "But won't that scare it off?"

"No," Jesse said. "It's trying to destroy the boat and I think when it strikes next it'll succeed."

Buckley blinked and without another word jumped into the captain's chair and fired up the engine. The boat shifted heavily to the right. The creature was attempting to tip them over.

"Hit it," Jesse shouted. "Now!"

Buckley shoved the throttle all the way up. The boat jolted forward so hard Jesse and Becca lost their balance and tumbled into the wall. Jesse held Becca so she wasn't flung around too bad and guided her to a chair and buckled her in.

"Oh, shit," Buckley shouted.

Jesse glanced over his shoulder, eyes widening. In the high-beams of the boat the monster reared out of the water, mouth gaping. Its eyes gleamed with carnage. The water appeared to boil around its partially submerged dark gray body.

Buckley turned the wheel, though not sharp enough, to veer away from the creature.

"We're gonna hit it," Jesse said. "Turn!"

"If I turn too sharp with the boat going this fast," Buckley said, "it could roll and capsize."

Jesse gaped at the monster as the boat, though turning slowly, surged toward that mouth filled with long, pointy teeth. In the intense light, it didn't look so much like a plesiosaurus than a serpent. Its head reminded him of a rattlesnake, though void of long fangs. The teeth were misplaced and jagged. That, at least, resembled the pictures of a plesiosaurus or mosasaurus Jesse remembered from school.

"We're gonna hit it," Jesse said. "Hang on!"

Buckley, despite no doubt knowing a collision was imminent, tried steering the boat farther to the left and slowing the speed. But it just wasn't enough. They were heading directly at the creature fast.

The monster bellowed.

"Hold on," Buckley shouted into the ship's mic and snapped into the chair's harness.

Jesse didn't like the idea of being locked into a chair with the possibility of sinking, but the impact was going to be nasty. He sat beside Becca and buckled in. He glanced at her and held her hand in his.

"If it gets bad," Jesse said, "stick close to me. We're on the life-pod out of here."

Her hand squeezed his. Hard. Her entire body straightened…eyes wide.

Jesse glanced at the windshield just as the boat collided with the monster of the Loch.

His entire world slammed forward and if not for the seat belt, he would have shot right through the windshield. Water slashed the windows. A loud squeal broke through the thundering of the collision. The boat shuddered violently then fell still.

Buckley groaned. "Y'all okay?"

Jesse clenched his jaw against the pain from the seat belt cutting into his waist and shoulder. He noticed how limp Becca's hand was in his and snapped his gaze at her. She sat, head down, mouth open...eyes closed. A pool of vomit soaked into the lap of her jeans.

"Hey," Jesse said and got out of his seat belt. He cupped Becca's cheeks in his hand and lifted her head gently. "Becca? Hey, hun. Wake up."

She shivered. Her eyelids fluttered.

"Ah, shit," Buckley said. "Think we might start sinkin' soon."

Jesse glanced at the captain. "How do you know?"

Buckley snorted. "I'm a captain, hoss. When the boat feels different, I notice. It feels different. Slanted. Not much. But we are sinkin'."

"We need to get—"

Someone screamed. A bunch of shouting followed. Then the pattering of a machine gun.

Jesse carefully lowered Becca's head, stood, and stared out of the windshield. For a second or two, he couldn't breathe. Eventually, he sucked in a breath, blew it out and looked at Buckley. "Can you get her into the life pod for me? Also, what's that dive suit do?"

"Yeah." Buckley frowned. "Dive sui—oh! Yep. Russians put it there. Said it's supposed to be shark-proof. Talkin' great white bite pressure. I think they said it has a gun mount for one of the arms too."

"So...it's kind of like a mech-suit?"

Buckley shrugged. "I guess? They told me it was in case the monster sinks the boat I'm to use the suit to eliminate it and—wait, where ya goin?"

Without looking back, Jesse opened the wheelhouse door. "To kill a monster."

23

The boat was indeed sinking. Slowly, but sinking, nonetheless. About half an inch of water skimmed the floor below deck.

"You are going in the water with it?" Uri frowned at Jesse.

Jesse snorted. "I know. I think I'm crazy too." He frowned at the suit, trying to figure out how to get the damn thing on. It stood at least a foot taller than him. Its width was another foot or so wider than his frame. The thing made his bowels churn a bit.

"It is a prototype," Uri said.

"Yeah," Jesse said and chuckled. "Thanks for the reminder. Help me roll this thing on deck."

Uri shook his head yet unhooked the suit and rolling trolley from the wall and floor. "Insane," he muttered under his breath.

Jesse grunted but couldn't disagree. What he was about to do was absolute insanity.

They wheeled the suit to the deck as the other crew members scurried about getting ready to abandon ship.

"The hell is that thing?" Becca said.

Jesse turned. Becca and Buckley stood about ten feet away. After she put two and two together, her eyes widened.

"You're not actually thinking about getting in the water with that thing?"

Jesse shrugged. "I mean, someone has to keep it busy while you all escape, right?"

Becca shook her head. Tears shimmered in her eyes. She gestured at a few of the crew members running around. "Have one of *them* do it. You don't always have to be the hero, Jesse."

He chuckled and finally figured out how to open the suit. "You know I'm no hero." He frowned at the inside of the suit. "If we all jump in the escape pod and cruise to shore, it'll catch us and kill us before we even come close to shore." He looked at Becca. "You just get to shore. I'll be right behind you."

Before Becca could protest, Buckley whisked her away.

Well, almost.

She shoved Buckley aside and stormed the ten or so feet to Jesse. "Listen, you stubborn son of a bitch." She jabbed a finger at his chest. "You're the only family I got left and if you die out there—"

Jesse pulled her into a firm embrace. She struggled, but only for a couple of seconds. Her arms slipped around his waist and tightened into a returned embrace. She laid her head on his chest and together they just breathed for a moment. After a bit, she let him go and stepped away.

"Just don't die on me," Becca said. She spun and walked away with Buckley before Jesse could respond.

He clenched his jaw and watched until she disappeared below deck.

"Need help with this?" Uri patted the dive suit.

Although dive suit was an understatement. The thing was, more or less, a mech.

"I...I'm not sure," Jesse said. "Never seen one of these things before."

Uri nodded. "Buckley knows."

"Can you get him for me?"

Again, Uri nodded. He jogged away and ducked below deck, leaving Jesse to stare out at the dark waters of Loch Ness. Did the collision injure the creature? God, he hoped so. It would make ending all of this so much easier. A part of him also hoped they scared it away.

He stared at the opened dive suit. Honestly, he didn't want to be trapped in that thing.

"Uri says ya got a question 'bout the dive suit?" Buckley said as he walked across the deck to Jesse.

"Yeah," Jesse said and chuckled humorlessly. "Like how does this damn thing work?"

"Man, I don't know everything," Buckley said. "Just basic controls, I guess." He shrugged. "They didn't give me any training or anything."

Jesse sighed. "You got a cigarette?"

Buckley laughed and clapped Jesse on the back. "Yup." He brought out a crumpled pack of Marlboros, shook two out, and handed Jesse one. "Didn't think you were a smoker." He lit Jesse's cigarette for him.

Jesse blew out a jet of smoke. "Off and on." He pointed at the dive suit. "How do I operate this thing?"

Buckley lit his own cigarette and nodded. "Once you're locked in, it's all verbal. You tell the thing what to do, like Alexa, right? Only it carries out everything you tell it. Just make sure your commands are precise, otherwise it'll do weird shit."

Jesse frowned. "Weird shit? Like what?"

"They told me if it misinterprets a command it'll try to destroy itself or completely shutdown. So, you'd be stuck in the thing until your oxygen ran out at the bottom of the lake."

"Gee, that makes me feel so much better," Jesse said. "Thanks, buddy."

Buckley coughed on his cigarette smoke laughing. Once he caught his breath, Buckley, still chuckling a bit, pointed at the dive suit. "All ya gotta do is tell it what to do. Just make sure the commands are clear. Tell it to dive. Tell it to swim, which it doesn't really swim but uses some kind of propulsion system. You can tell it how fast to go and all that."

"Okay. Does it go by miles per hour or knots...or?"

The man blinked. "Oh, hell, I can't remember. I think...I *think* it goes by kilometers per hour."

"I don't know kilometers per hour, though. I'm not even sure how to convert that to miles per hour."

Buckley shrugged. "Pretty simple, though. Ya just multiply the number you want by 0.62 to miles per hour."

Jesse stared blankly at Buckley for a few seconds. "Oh, for fuck sake. I'm not gonna remember that. Is there an English setting or something?"

"Um, maybe?" Buckley shrugged. "Once you're in there ask if it can translate to English?"

"Okay," Jesse said. "I'm not doing this." He gestured to the suit. "You staying on the boat?"

Buckley frowned. "It's sinkin'. Why would I stay?"

"Aren't captains supposed to go down with the ship?"

"Nah." Buckley waved a dismissive hand. "That's a myth and this isn't a ship. It's a damn yacht, to be honest. A boat."

Jesse rolled his eyes. "So, you're a coward. Got it."

That bristled Buckley a bit. "Coward? I ain't no coward, asshole."

Jesse smiled. "Stop it. I'm kidding."

The young captain rolled his eyes. "Anyway, either ya get in that suit or come with us." He stomped on the deck. "Cause she's goin' down."

Jesse stared at the dive suit. "That thing just feels like a really bad idea."

"Then don't—"

The monster burst out of the water and crashed into the side of the boat hard enough to knock both men off their feet. The boat reared and the cart holding the dive suit rolled across the deck and slammed into the right railing. The boat fell back and rocked a bit before going relatively still again. Now, however, evidence of the vessel sinking was front and center. The deck slanted toward the bow where Loch Ness began trickling in.

"Holy shit," Buckley shouted and scrambled to his feet. "She's still alive!"

"Yeah," Jesse said and pointed toward the door to below deck. "Go check on everyone in the pod."

Buckley nodded and started in that direction when the creature slipped out of the darkness and lunged over the bow. It snapped its jaws at Buckley, narrowly missing the man. Jesse detached the left machine gun and swung around so fast he about fell. The gun itself was heavy as hell, but he managed to lift it long enough to fire a few rounds into the gray hide of the monster.

It shrieked, once more missing Buckley with its snapping jaws, and whipped around to face Jesse. Jesse dropped the heavy machine gun, drew his pistol and shot it in the face. The monster shrieked and swung its head away. Without pause, Jesse sprinted across the deck, shoved Buckley toward the door that led to below deck, and spun the dive suit around.

He stopped long enough to glance at the creature. It shook its head and glared directly at him. Blood trickled down the slope of its face.

"Ah, shit," Jesse said and was about to skip the dive suit and run when the creature lashed one of its giant flippers at him.

Jesse stumbled backward into the suit. It hissed. Something beeped.

"Oh, shi—"

Before he could jump out...the dive suit sealed itself around him.

For a second or two he stood in complete darkness. The only sounds were of his own breathing and the thudding of his heart. Panic began to set in then a gentle hiss and cool air filled the suit. A bunch of lights flickered on. An artificial voice said something in obvious Russian.

"Uh," Jesse said. "Hi?"

A series of beeps, then a long silence followed. He was about to say something to break the silence, when the suit released a long beep. A deep noise vibrated the suit and a sense of motion followed. Like when an elevator descends.

"We are sinking," an AI voice said in English. "Twenty feet and falling." A pause. "Do you wish to activate stabilization?"

"Yes," Jesse nearly shouted and once again came the sensation of being in an elevator, this time of one coming to a stop.

"We are stabilized at sixty-four feet below the surface," the AI said. "Do you wish to swim?"

"No," Jesse said, heart bashing itself against his ribs. "Not yet. Just...just give me a second."

"Your heart rate is alarmingly high."

Jesse chuckled. "Gee, thanks for reminding me." He took a few slow breaths. He considered himself lucky, though. The suit hadn't misunderstood him yet and shutdown. There was that.

Once his nerves eased and his breathing slowed, Jesse glanced around the suit. There wasn't much room to move around, but just enough to get a sense of the contraption keeping him alive under water.

In front of him were three small screens. The center one was a bit larger than the peripherals. They were all dark.

"A large mass is approaching," the AI said, startling Jesse.

"Um..." For a second, Jesse's brain stuttered. He blinked at the dark screen in front of him. "Um...get out of its way."

"Do we wish to swim?"

"Oh, for fuck sake," Jesse said. "Yes!"

"Explain, 'for fuck sake'," the AI said.

Jesse clamped his mouth shut, not sure how to proceed.

"Do we wish to swim?"

He cleared his throat. "Yes." And sort of off handedly, "Wish I could see too."

Again, that elevator sensation. Only instead of up and down it was to the side.

"We are swimming at fifteen miles per hour," the AI said.

"Oh, thank god," Jesse said. "You know miles per hour."

"Yes," the AI said. "We are using the English language." A pause. "Do we wish to swim faster? The large mass is now forty-one feet away."

"Yes," Jesse said, then thought about it. "No. Dive. Do you understand dive?"

"Yes," the AI said. "I understand. Preparing to dive. At what speed do we wish to dive?"

"Eighty miles per hour," Jesse said. "Can I see too?"

A pause. "Please rephrase the last question." This was quickly followed by, "Large mass is now fifteen feet from our location."

Jesse's heart stuttered. "Dive at eighty miles per hour. Now!"

"Diving," the AI said, and the suit bent and moved around Jesse.

He followed the movements of the suit.

"We are descending at eighty miles per hour. Seventy-six feet to the loch's floor."

Thoughts raced through his brain at speed so rapid he couldn't catch any of them until the suit's AI said, "Do we wish to stabilize at sixty feet?"

Jesse blinked. "Um…yes. Sixty feet. Why can't I see?"

"I don't understand the question. Please rephrase."

Jesse clenched his jaw. "These screens in front of me. Turn them on."

A long pause. "Do you wish to establish vision?"

"Oh for the love of—*yes*! Establish vision."

The small screens in front of him flickered on and gave him the current view outside of the suit. Which wasn't much of anything except for silvery bubbles and the darkness of Loch Ness. Jesse stared at the screen in front of him, momentarily stunned. Everything that had happened up until now rolled over him like a giant boulder and for a few seconds he couldn't breathe.

"You have not taken a breath in twenty seconds," the AI said. "If you wish resuscitation, please nod."

Jesse finally sucked in a deep breath and gradually began to breathe regularly.

"Do you wish to surface?"

"No," Jesse said after a bit. "No. H-How far from the floor are we?"

"Twenty-eight feet. Speed is decreasing now. We will stabilize at ten feet from the floor."

Jesse stared at the screen in front of him. He turned his head left and right a few centimeters and caught a burst of bubbles from the right.

"Where is the large mass?" he said.

"Sixty-seven feet above, moving west," the AI said.

Jesse frowned. "Is the mass chasing something?"

A long pause. So long, Jesse was about to yell at the suit, when it said, "Yes. Our life pod."

"Shit." Jesse's heart thrummed. "We need to stop it."

"Which should we stop?"

"The creature," Jesse said. "Hurry, we gotta—"

"Do you wish to stop the large mass?"

Jesse gritted his teeth against a roar, swallowed it down, and said, "Yes! Stop the large mass, for fuck sake."

"We do not understand 'fuck sake'. Please rephrase."

"Oh, for the love of—Yes. Stop the large mass. Swim as fast as you can."

"Top speed?"

"Yes!"

"Do you wish to collide with the large mass?"

"Whatever," Jesse said. "Just go!"

In less than a second, the pressure in the suit increased. His boots pressed against the feet of the suit.

"Stabilizing pressure to accommodate speed," the AI said. "Do you wish to unalive the large mass?"

Jesse opened his mouth and closed it again. What did it mean, exactly? How was it going to kill Nessie? How? As far as he knew, the suit didn't have any weapons equipped.

"Um..." Jesse fell into a loss of words. He wasn't sure, once again, how to engage the AI. "So...how would you, uh, unalive the mass?"

"We are forty feet from the large mass," the AI said. "To answer your question, we can unalive the mass via cutting torch or knife built into our system."

"You have a knife and torch?"

"Yes." The AI paused. "We are now twenty feet away from the mass."

Jesse blinked and stared at the screen in front of him. So far, though, he didn't see anything.

"Ten feet," the AI said. "Do you wish to—"

"The knife," Jesse said just as the monster came into view. "Use the knife to unalive the mass."

The AI didn't say anything, so Jesse hoped it understood the command.

The monster was in full view now. Well, at least half of it and holy shit it was massive. Much larger than Jesse imagined. Its long tail moved back and forth, much like a great white shark. Slow. Deliberate. Constant. From there he caught a large flipper, though nothing smooth like paddles. They appeared to have claws or curved talons at the end like hooks. The rear flippers didn't sport much of those, but the front ones did.

"Preparing to unalive mass," the AI said. "Knife deployed."

"Here we go," Jesse whispered and braced himself.

The suit began to move, shift, and he moved with it. The scene in front of him was nothing but the creature and millions of silvery bubbles flying by as if he was going warp speed through space and bubbles were stars.

"Initiating unalive mode," the AI said.

The suit swooped upward, right arm extended. Jesse looked up to see the underside of the monster. The suit, with Jesse allowing it to move him, stabbed the knife into the underside of the creature and powered forward, slicing through the tough hide as it went. It was literally disemboweling the Loch Ness Monster.

"Holy shit," Jesse said.

It was over in less than five seconds.

The suit blasted away from the monster towards the life pod. Its speed slowed gradually.

"We are twenty feet from our life pod," the AI said. "The mass has been unalived. Do you wish to accompany our life pod to shore?"

Jesse sighed relief. "Yes. Good job."

The AI paused for a few seconds. "You are welcome."

Not far ahead, Jesse saw the first glimpse of the life pod.

24

"Would you like us to contact the life pod?"

Jesse blinked. "Sure."

"Please reword."

Jesse sighed. "Yes. Contact the life—"

"Large mass approach—"

Jesse was knocked around inside the suit a bit. Just enough to know something was seriously wrong. The screens were a mess of bubbles. It was like he was in a washing machine. Something beeped repeatedly.

"We are in a wake," the AI said in its uninterested monotone. "Do you wish to leave the wake?"

"Yes," Jesse said without hesitation through his gritted teeth. He wanted to add more explicative language but managed to refrain. Barely.

In about a minute, the rocking and knocking and beeping stopped. He didn't feel like he was trapped in a washing machine anymore and frowned at the screens in front of him, which were utterly black.

"What's happening?"

"We are evaluating our situation," the AI said. "Please stand by."

"Lovely," Jesse said, mind reeling with the possibility of the life pod exploding or something worse. His heart ached even at the thought of losing Becca.

"No damages," the AI said. "The large mass has disappeared."

"What about the life pod?" Jesse's heart hammered.

"Our life pod has reached its destination on shore."

Jesse released a long breath, too heavy to be a sigh. "Thank God." He took a few slow breaths until the hammering of his heart eased and frowned at the screen in front of him. Nothing but darkness and bubbles out there. "Any signs of the large mass?"

"No," the AI said. "Mass is most likely unalived."

"Okay," Jesse said. He thought about it a bit. "Is there a way to scan Loch Ness…just to be sure?"

"Yes. Do you wish us to swim the entirety of Loch Ness?"

"How long would that take?"

The AI paused for a few seconds. "For a complete scan of the entire loch…" It paused for another few seconds. "Three hours or less, depending on speed."

"What time is it now?"

"3:47 AM."

So, it would be after six o'clock when they would be finished with the scans. Yeah, no.

"Okay," Jesse said. "Let's go to shore."

A long pause followed.

"My programming details I must not seek shore until the mass is unalived."

Jesse frowned. "What?"

"My programming details I must—"

"I heard you the first time," Jesse said. "So, my commands don't matter now?"

"You are not my programmer. Laws of the programmer trumps the commands of the diver. And my direct orders come from the programmer to be sure the mass is unalived."

"Wait, I thought your people wanted to capture it?" Jesse glanced from the screen in front of him to the right peripheral. "You're not supposed to kill it."

"Our main vessel has been destroyed," the AI said. "Fall back programming dictates death for the mass."

"I don't suppose you can drop me off at shore first?"

"No."

Jesse sighed. "Fine. Let's do this" He shook his head. "Not like I have a choice anyway."

"Preparing lifeform sensors," the AI said. "Do you wish to listen to music while we scan Loch Ness?"

If there was an AI face to punch right now, Jesse would bash its nose in.

"Your heart rate is rising," the AI said.

"Just…" Jesse clenched his jaw for a second and shook his head. "Just scan the fucking loch."

"Your body temperature is rising. Do you wish to engage the cooling system?"

"Is that like air conditioning?"

"Yes."

Jesse snorted. "Then that's a definite yes. Getting a bit stuffy in here."

"Stuffy?"

Jesse rolled his eyes. "Never mind. Just cool it down in here a little."

A low hiss filled the suit followed by cool air that slithered around his sweaty skin. He sighed in relief, not realizing just how hot it had gotten. He couldn't hate the suit. It was just doing what it was programmed to do. Jesse focused his hatred at the Russian programmers.

Another thing he hated was not being able to wipe sweat from his face, which was irritating the hell out of him.

As if reading his mind, a cool breeze swept across his forehead, drying the sweat.

He grunted. He hated the thought of using AI as a crutch for anything, but…this one appeared it could be more human than humans at times. A bit uncanny. A lot unnerving. Not like he had a choice anyway. He was trapped in the suit until it let him out.

"With no obstructions," the AI said, "our speed to the northern point of Loch Ness will be one hundred miles per hour. When we begin to scan, our top speed will be twenty-five miles per hour."

"Oh, that's just fantastic," Jesse said.

"I note sarcasm in your tone."

"Damn, it was that obvious?"

A long pause followed. "We are sensing more sarcasm."

Jesse snorted. "Okay, okay. Let's just scan this lake and get it over with."

"It is called a loch in Scotland."

Jesse sighed and bit the inside of his cheek to stop himself from shouting at the AI. It wasn't a person and shouting wouldn't make it better anyway. Eventually, his anger slipped away, and he stared at the screen while the suit surged through the dark waters of Loch Ness.

In less than ten minutes, the AI announced, "We have reached the northernmost point of Loch Ness. Preparing to scan in a one-mile radius, which is the width of the loch."

"Great," Jesse said. "Let's get this over with."

Honestly, he had a good feeling the creature was dead or bleeding out at sea by now. Maybe a great white shark or something was finishing the job. Regardless, he didn't think the monster was still in the loch.

"We are moving south at twenty-five miles per hour and now approaching the twenty-meter mark."

Twenty meters. Which, if his math was correct, meant sixty-five feet or so. Maybe it wouldn't take as long as the AI predicted. Three hours? At this rate? Nah. Maybe two hours, give or take. But weren't AIs supposed to be all about facts?

"This is going to take three hours?"

"We will sweep Loch Ness twice," the AI said.

"Oh…" Jesse frowned. "Why twice?"

"To be one hundred percent accurate."

"Lovely," Jesse said and sighed.

"I detect sarcasm."

Jesse snorted, rolled his eyes and decided not to respond. Just getting it over with was all he cared about.

A long space of time rolled by. So long, he fell asleep for a bit. Nothing restful, but exhaustion was leeching away all his energy. Not to mention the AI suit was wasting time swimming around. They should just—

"We have reached the second pass of Loch Ness," the AI said.

Jesse sighed. "Lovely."

The AI didn't respond to his sarcasm this time. Which was just as well.

"We are now twenty meters from the northern shore," the AI said.

Jesse thought about taking another nap. He glanced at the screens in front of him and seeing nothing except dark waters sprinkled with bubbles, rolled his eyes and sighed heavily. Yeah, maybe a nap would—

Without warning a strong sense of vertigo struck him. He bounced against the inside of the suit a bit. Nothing hard enough to hurt, but still. What...

"Stabilizing," the AI said. "Large mass detected."

"Shit," Jesse said. "Where is it?"

"Twenty feet below us. Moving south at a speed we cannot detect."

"Can we catch it?"

"We should not engage yet."

Jesse frowned. "Why?"

"We need to scan its size and proportions to engage."

"What the hell are you—"

"Large mass approaching," the AI said.

"Wait...did you just interrupt me?"

"Yes," the AI said. "The large mass has been scanned. Do you wish to unalive it?"

"Do I wish—*yes*! Why would I want it alive? Kill that bastard."

"You are very profane," the AI said. "Please rephrase."

Jesse growled a bit. "Fine. Unalive the large mass." He wanted to add so much more but the damn AI was being an AI about everything.

"I hate technology," Jesse said.

"Do you wish to terminate us?"

Jesse blinked. "What?"

"Our sensors tell us you are angry with us."

Jesse cleared his throat. "Well, yeah. I don't want to be out here. I want—"

A dull thud and that sense of extreme vertigo again. So much so he nearly vomited. The screens revealed nothing but chaos so no help there. The suit beeped a couple of times.

"What's going on?"

The AI, however, didn't respond. And, again, a dull thud followed by vertigo. Like he was tumbling through space. Which, once he thought about it, was pretty damn close to the truth.

"Stabilizing," the AI said. "The large mass is attacking. We are evaluating possible scenarios and actions."

Jesse grunted. "Yeah? I mean, maybe we should kill it? Like really kill it this time?"

"Please refrain from sarcasm," the AI said.

"No," Jesse said, anger frothing. "Kill the fucking thing or I will."

A slight pause. "Do you wish to implement full control?"

Jesse opened his mouth, then closed it. Not sure how to respond. He had no clue how to pilot a dive-suit-mech-thing like this. No training. No—

"The large mass is about to attack again. Do you wish to implement full control?"

Jesse cleared his throat. "Will you be here to help me if I go full control?"

"No," the AI said. "Only voice command will be available. We will be offline."

"Okay," Jesse said and frowned. He thought about it a bit. "What about partial control?"

"Yes. We can give you partial control of the system and guide your commands. This is the recommended option."

"Well, shit," Jesse said. "Let's do that. Partial control, if you're there to help."

"Very well," the AI said. "You are now in partial control of Diver Suit 5."

A sudden jolt of vertigo, like on a falling elevator or a fast car speeding down a steep hill.

"What just happened?" Jesse said.

"We are sinking," the AI said, though its tone was different now. Less interested? Was that even possible?

The commands the AI used earlier rolled through Jesse's mind like a rolodex. The command he needed took a few minutes but...

"Stabilize?"

"Do not ask questions," the AI said. "Command."

Jesse cleared his throat. "Stabilize."

The reverse sensation of falling slammed through him. A sudden stop? Something like that.

"We are stabilized," the AI said.

Jesse released a breath he didn't know he'd been holding. He let his mind and nerves settle before saying anything. It took a bit and he thanked whatever gods were out there that the monster didn't attack while he gathered himself.

"Can we scan for the large mass?" His voice sounded so small inside of the suit.

"Yes," the AI said. "Do you wish to scan for the large mass now?"

"Yes."

"Scanning."

A sharp beep startled Jesse.

"Large mass closing in at high rate of speed."

"Shit," Jesse said. His mind froze for a second or two.

"Do you wish to evade a collision?" The AI almost sounded annoyed now.

"Um, yes. Evade a collision."

"Do you wish to dip, rise or dash in a different direction? Large mass collision imminent."

"Dash right," Jesse snapped.

Strong sense of vertigo.

"We have dashed fifty feet to the right and have avoided collision."

Jesse shivered. "Good. Is there a way I can see what's out there better?"

"Do you wish to expand viewing screens?"

"Yes," Jesse said without pause.

He gaped while the screens expanded, connected and surrounded the entire inside of the suit's head.

"Viewing expanded," the AI said. "You now have three hundred and sixty degrees viewing."

"How do I see behind me?"

"Command rearview."

Jesse grunted. "Rearview."

The screen in front of him jittered a bit, though it appeared the same. Vast darkness littered with tiny bubbles. Jesse sighed. But at least he could see in every direction now instead of regulated to the small screens. There was just one problem…

"Is there a way I can see better in the water?"

The AI didn't reply for a long minute then the view flickered. Instead of darkness and bubbles—a large pike swam by. His heart slammed into his throat. He gasped. Going from utter darkness to a fish directly in front of him was unexpected. He chuckled and let his nerves calm a bit. He turned his head and the suit followed his movements. Ah, so that's how that would work. All he needed to do was move and it worked with him.

"We can make the view clearer, if you wish," the AI said.

"Yes," Jesse said. "I want to be able to see—"

The view flickered again and staring directly at him through the murky, yellowish water, was the monster. Its eyes glimmered like diamonds.

"Large mass detected," the AI said.

Jesse snorted. "Ya think? How far away?"

"Eighty-two feet. Drifting closer at five miles per hour."

"What's it waiting for?" Jesse asked himself.

"It appears to be stalking us," the AI answered.

Jesse clenched his jaw and glared at the creature. His mind was a chaotic mess, but finally landed on a way forward. A plan, for lack of a better word. Although he wasn't exactly sure if he'd call it a plan. Maybe a tentative idea? Yeah. That.

"I want to unalive the large mass," Jesse said.

"Would you like to use the knife or torch?"

"Knife," Jesse said, glaring at the creature. "Swim at one hundred miles per hour at the mass's neck."

"A swim so fast could injure you if there is a collision."

Jesse nodded. "Then we better not collide with the thing." He thought about it. "Can you control the speed and steering while I control using the knife?"

The AI didn't say anything for at least a minute.

Finally, it said, "Yes."

"Okay. Good. I want you to swim at one hundred miles per hour to its neck. Get me directly under it. Dodge any actions on its part. Don't stop until we are a safe distance away."

Again, the AI took about a minute to respond.

"Confirmed."

Jesse drew in a slow breath and blew it out. "Okay. Let's do this."

The monster, still closing in, opened its large mouth and closed it again.

"Engaging in...3...2...1."

A massive sensation knocked Jesse back a bit inside the suit. Through the viewer surrounding his head he watched the monster get closer and closer really fast.

"Shit," Jesse said, wondering if he had made a mistake. He was going too fast and wasn't ready with the knife. Hell, he wasn't even sure which arm the knife would be in.

No way to stop it now.

"Dipping under mass's neck now," the AI announced.

Yes, they were indeed dipping down. Jesse glanced to his left, but there wasn't a knife on that arm.

"Okay," he said, and using his right arm, he stabbed the knife into the creature's throat.

The blade sliced through the thick skin, spilling a rooster tail of blood behind him as the suit darted out of the monster's range. It slowed, stopped and turned around so Jesse could see the Loch Ness Monster.

It writhed, lashed its head back and forth while a thick cloud of blood engulfed it. So much blood, Jesse couldn't see the thing anymore.

"The mass is dying," the AI said. "Congratulations."

"Hold the champagne until we see the body."

The AI did not respond.

"Swim around the blood at twenty-five miles per hour and scan for the mass," Jesse said.

The suit moved closer toward the blood cloud. He shivered in anticipation and hope. Let it be over. Let it be over n—

It blasted out of the blood at Jesse so fast he didn't have time to command the suit. It struck, spinning him around. He was just gathering his thoughts when it struck again. This time swinging its massive head around and clamping its toothy mouth around the suit and Jesse. A few loud beeps assaulted his ears.

"What's happening?" Jesse said.

"We have a pressure warning," the AI said. "There is a shallow puncture near our left shoulder."

"Is it life threatening?"

A long pause.

Finally, the AI said, "Not an imminent threat."

"How long before it becomes a serious threat?"

"One hour," the AI said. "Unless more punctures occur."

"Okay," Jesse said, trying to ignore the sweat trickling down his face and the urge to wipe it away. He turned his head and the suit moved with him.

He stared down the throat of the Loch Ness Monster.

"Shit," Jesse said and glanced at the long teeth gripping him.

"Do you wish to counter the mass's attack?" The AI sounded almost bored now.

"Working on it," Jesse said and looked at the large knife protruding from the suit's right arm. "When the mouth opens, swim away at one hundred miles per hour."

"Do you wish to dash out of the mouth first?"

"What's the difference?"

"A dash is faster," the AI said.

"Yeah," Jesse said. "Yeah, dash first then get away from the mass as fast as possible."

"Confirmed."

Jesse grunted and stabbed the blade into the top of the monster's mouth. The creature swung him back and forth but didn't let go.

"Goddamn it," Jesse said while the suit beeped alarms at him.

"The mass has not released us," the AI said. "Outside pressure is increasing. Another puncture imminent."

Shit, Jesse thought. *Shit, shit, shit, sh—*

His gaze fixed on the creature's thick tongue. He smiled.

"Get ready to dash," he told the AI.

"Confirmed."

Jesse lifted his right arm, drew in a breath, and swung the knife downward. The blade sliced through the tongue. Blood spurted, filling the monster's mouth and...

The jaws opened and the suit dashed out of the huge mouth and into open water. Before Jesse could get a good look at the creature, the suit jetted away at one hundred miles per hour.

"We are sixty feet from the mass," the AI announced. "Do you wish to stop?"

"No," Jesse said. "Swing back around." He glared at the rush of water, fish, and bubbles. "Let's end this."

"We are damaged," the AI said. "Another attack will mean termination for us and you will be unalived."

"Can I set up an emergency request?"

The AI paused, then beeped. After another few seconds, it said, "Yes."

"If termination is close," Jesse said, "expel me from this suit."

"At what depth?" the AI said. "If too deep you will drown."

"Ten feet," Jesse said without hesitation. "Max."

The AI didn't respond. Once again, he hoped it understood. He guessed he'd find out either way in the end. Which didn't sit well with his anxiety thinking about it. Still...

"Swing back around to the mass," Jesse said.

"Confirmed."

The suit swept right and darted back toward the monster.

25

By the time he arrived at the spot, which was still clouded with blood, the monster was gone.

"What are the scans saying?" Jesse asked the AI.

"Small lifeforms are swarming us," the AI said. "There is no sign of the large mass."

"Fuck," Jesse said. He turned around and the suit moved with him. There were several fish swimming about, but no Loch Ness Monster.

His heart thrummed. The creature was alive, hurt…but alive. An eerie stirring in his gut told him that much. A feeling he had learned to listen to over the years because it was often spot on. The question was…where did the damn thing go?

"All scans show no large mass within a one hundred feet radius," the AI said.

Jesse sighed heavily and tried to think of where the creature would swim off to.

"Do you wish to scan the entire loch?"

"Yes," Jesse said without hesitation. "Let's find this bastard."

"It is 3:30 am," the AI said. "Sunrise is 4:33 am in Scotland during June."

"Yeah, we don't want to be here during daylight," Jesse said.

"My programming acknowledges this." The AI paused. "Do you wish to do a full scan of Loch Ness?"

"Yes, but make it quick." He sighed. "We might have to come back tomorr—"

"Our time is less than one hour to scan the loch," the AI interrupted. "If you do not wish to scan Loch Ness then I need a different command."

"Damn," Jesse said. "What's with the attitude?"

"I do not have an attitude," the AI said.

"Uh, yeah…that was definitely major attitude."

The AI fell silent.

Jesse snorted. "Anyway, yes. Let's scan the loch."

"Confirmed."

They sped through the dark waters scanning in a one-hundred-foot radius as they went. About half an hour later and the scans revealed no monster, the AI said, "It is possible the mass escaped Loch Ness."

"Through the tunnels?"

"Yes."

Jesse frowned. "Would it more likely escape to the ocean or another loch?"

"There are more predators in the ocean," the AI said. "The mass is injured and bleeding…"

"Right. So, it must be in another loch. But which one?"

It took the AI a few minutes to respond. "The most likely lochs the mass would escape to are: Loch Oich, Loch Garry, and Loch Morar."

"Why only those?"

"Partly seclusion and deeper water to hide in and heal."

Jesse nodded. "How long will it take us to get to Loch Oich?"

"Less than an hour."

"Loch Garry?"

"An hour or hour and a half. Loch Morar is farther away and will take at least two hours."

"Well, shit," Jesse said. "I guess we're going on an adventure."

"Do you wish to scan Loch Oich now?"

Jesse clenched his jaw. "As soon as—"

"Large mass approaching," the AI blurted.

Jesse's heart slammed into his throat. "What? It—"

"Approaching at more than fifty miles per hour. ETA in ten seconds."

"Dash to the right," Jesse said. "Then swim at one hundred miles per hour away from the mass."

"Confirmed."

The suit dashed and—

The monster slammed into the suit so hard it jarred Jesse inside a bit. His forehead smacked the viewer.

"Shit," Jesse said, grimacing from the pain spreading along his forehead and the extreme sense of vertigo. Like he was trapped on a Tilt-o-Whirl.

"We are spinning," the AI said.

"Yeah," Jesse said, trying not to vomit. "Stabilize."

The spinning sensation gradually stopped, and he was thankful the suit didn't just stop the spinning without slowing it first. A sudden stop might have turned his insides into Jell-O.

"The large mass is approaching," the AI said.

"Which direction?" Jesse said.

"Incoming from the north."

Jesse, using the suit's compass, turned north. But even with his enhanced vision through the viewer all he saw were various fish. A few weeds floated and rippled like ghosts. He glanced toward the surface but there was nothing there.

"Where the hell is it?"

The AI didn't reply. In fact, it went utterly silent on him.

Jesse sucked in a sharp breath as if slapped and looked down into the depths of Loch Ness. It was like staring into an endless, dark abyss. Silence, except for his own breathing, filled the suit.

"Where is the mass?" Jesse said.

"Not detecting a large mass right now," the AI said.

Jesse blinked. "So, what…it just disappeared?"

The AI didn't reply.

He was about to tell the suit to swim for the nearest tunnel when suddenly the darkness below him opened up, revealing a large, open mouth filled with teeth.

"Oh, shi—dash left!"

The suit dashed him to the left, though not far enough. The monster's lower jaw struck his right leg and sent him pinwheeling through the water.

"Stabilize," Jesse shouted while trying once again not to vomit. The suit gradually stopped pinwheeling. Once he was stable, he glanced around but the creature was nowhere in sight. That didn't mean anything though.

He felt it lurking just out of sight. A shiver trickled along his spine. He wanted nothing more than to speed to shore, despite the AI...

Wait.

"Swim one hundred miles per hour to shore," Jesse said.

The AI didn't reply, and the suit began moving.

Then stopped abruptly.

"My creator's programming does not allow us to return to shore until the mass is destroyed."

"Override," Jesse said.

"The override command was disabled by the creator."

"I am the creator," Jesse said. "Override."

"You are not our creator," the AI said. "The override command was disabled by the creator."

Jesse grunted. "So, your creator would rather have you terminated than trying another day?"

"Yes."

"Then let's kill this thing, for fuck sake." He was hoping the override trick would have worked, but alas...

"We do not detect the large mass."

"Oh, it's out there," Jesse said. He looked around. "Waiting for the right moment." His heart thrummed at the very thought of the monster stalking him.

He waited a few minutes and when nothing happened, Jesse said, "Swim to where the boat sank."

The AI didn't say anything for another minute or so. "What is your objective?"

Jesse frowned. "To bait the mass. Like a fishing lure." That's not exactly why, but it sounded good and hopefully the AI would understand.

"We are bait?"

"Yep," Jesse said.

"That objective does not seem safe."

"None of this shit is safe," Jesse said, trying not to shout.

"Returning to the boat would be counterproductive."

Jesse thought up a quick lie. "I left my journal in there. There might be a way to kill the large mass."

The AI didn't say anything for a bit. "If your journal is paper, it will not be viable."

"It's..." Jesse blinked and sucked in a sharp breath as if slapped.

"Large mass detected," the AI said.

"No shit."

Floating no more than twenty feet away, the monster glared directly at him through the gloom of Loch Ness. Without the enhanced viewer he would not have known how close it was. Maybe that would have been better than seeing the creature so damn close, its eyes glinting and its long teeth overlapping the lower and upper jaws. And all it did was float there...watching him. It didn't move. Didn't even blink. Tendrils of blood seeped through the gaps between its teeth.

"Do you wish to swim?" the AI said.

Jesse snorted. "Do you think we'll make it with the mass being so close?" He still hated calling it a mass, but apparently that was what the AI knew it as.

"Yes," the AI said. "Dash down thirty feet and swim two hundred miles per hour in any direction."

"Two hundred?" Jesse said, eyes widening. "You can go that fast?"

"Our top speed is three hundred miles per hour."

"Well, that would have been useful to know like an hour ago."

"We sense sarcasm," the AI said.

Jesse chuckled. "Oh, stop it." He laughed a little and cleared his throat. If he let the laughter go too long, it might end up taking over. The very realization of that sent rills of terror through him.

"Do you have a command?" the AI said.

"Dash down twenty feet and dash two hundred miles per hour toward the boat."

"The boat is counterproductive."

"Just do it," Jesse said, and, for a wonder, the AI didn't argue.

The suit slipped downward, and Jesse lost sight of the monster for a handful of terrorizing seconds. He spotted it just as the suit jetted away. He wasn't sure if it was taking him toward the sunken boat or not. Maybe that was for the best. Maybe. He just wanted to get them closer to shore. He wanted this to be over. One way or another.

The suit slowed to a stop and stabilized.

"Where are we?"

"Near the boat," the AI said.

"Are you lying?"

"No."

Jesse grunted, though he wasn't sure he believed the AI. He looked around but didn't see a sunken boat anywhere.

"I don't see the boat."

"That is because we are eighty feet away," the AI said. "The water is too murky, even for the enhanced view."

"Well, excuse me all to hell," Jesse said.

The AI didn't respond. Probably for the best. The damn thing was getting on Jesse's nerves. Because even though it was factual and all, its tone kept getting snarkier and snarkier. He glanced around for the creature, but there was no sign. Well, at least not yet.

"Any trace of the large mass yet?"

"No," the AI said.

An idea flashed through Jesse's mind right then. "The harpoon…"

"Please explain what you mean by harpoon?"

"We need to get to the boat," Jesse said, mind reeling.

"The boat is not productive."

"It is now," Jesse said. "We need to get to the harpoon."

A few seconds floated by. "Why do you need the harpoon?"

Jesse stared into the darkness of Loch Ness. "To slay a dragon, you need a lance."

The AI didn't respond and the suit began to move.

26

The boat appeared like a ghost from the bottom of the loch as Jesse approached.

The suit stopped directly above the bow and Jesse spotted the harpoon right away.

"Okay," Jesse said. "Let's swim to the harpoon and—"

"Large mass approaching," the AI said.

"How close?"

"Forty feet nd closing," the AI. "Cannot detect speed."

"Okay, let's get the harpoon."

"You referenced a dragon and a lance earlier," the AI said.

Jesse blinked. "I did, but I don't think we have time to—"

"That reference confused us until we researched it." The AI paused for a moment and added, "We now understand."

"Cool," Jesse said. "Can we get the harpoon now?"

The suit rushed to the bow's harpoon.

"The harpoon is secured and cannot be taken out without firing the gun it is located in."

"So be it," Jesse said. "Let's—"

"Collision with large mass is imminent."

"Swim to the harpoon gun," Jesse shouted. "Now!"

The suit rushed to the harpoon gun just as the monster whooshed by overhead.

"The large mass is circling," the AI said.

"Okay," Jesse said and, using the suit, grabbed onto the harpoon gun and swiveled it around. "Let's bag us the Loch Ness Monster."

"Do you mean unalive?"

Jesse sighed. "Yeah. Unalive. Whatever."

"We sense sarcasm."

Jesse chuckled and glanced around for the monster.

"We lost detection of the large mass," the AI said. "Do you wish to stay with the boat?"

"Yes," Jesse said. "This ends now."

He swiveled around slowly until the harpoon stopped about a foot away from pointing at the boat.

"Well, that might be a problem," he said to himself.

"There is a swivel lock," the AI said. "To prevent injury to the crew aboard."

"Okay. How do I release the lock?"

"There is a—large mass approaching fast."

Jesse blinked. "Which direction?"

"East. Moving no less than fifty miles per hour."

Jesse swiveled the harpoon gun eastward, squinting a bit. "Can the viewer be enhanced more?"

"No. You are at maximum view."

"Lovely." Jesse continued to squint and kept his focus east. Still no sign of the creature yet.

Loch Ness stilled. No weeds floated like ghosts, nor the casual fish swimming by. Hell, if not for the bubbles, he might as well be trapped in a motionless void.

"The large mass has disappeared," the AI said.

"What?" Jesse said. "Are you fucking kidding me? I thought it was speeding at us?"

"It was," the AI said. "We lost detection sixty feet rom our location."

Jesse shook his head and looked around. Something finally dawned on him just then. In McComb's journal, he mentioned the creature was spliced with some kind of species that could camouflage itself. The name of the species eluded Jesse, though. Was it the cuttlefish? Yeah. Maybe it was the cuttlefish.

"It's camouflaging itself," Jesse said. "That's why you can't detect it. Try a different kind of scan. Thermal, or—"

"Switched to thermal scanning," the AI said. Paused. "The large mass is suspended at seventy feet away to the east and fifty feet deep."

"How far will the harpoon reach?"

"Sixty feet," the AI replied.

"Goddamn it," Jesse said and glared in the direction of the creature. "We gotta get it closer to the boat."

"Do you wish to leave the harpoon gun?"

Jesse clenched his jaw, thinking. He didn't want to leave or stray too far from the harpoon gun. The creature could move fast and strike without warning. The harpoon could be the only thing that might subdue the monster. And once it was subdued, he would finish the job. But how the hell was he going to get it close enough?

"Large mass is drifting closer," the AI said. "Less than two miles per hour."

"Let's wait and see what it's going to do," Jesse said, focus trained eastward.

"We still do not understand the significance of the harpoon," the AI said. "You cannot use it like a lance. You must shoot it."

"Yeah," Jesse said. "I used an analogy of using a lance against a dragon." He smiled. "Doesn't matter how the lance or harpoon kills the dragon."

The AI didn't say anything for a full minute or so. "We understand."

"Good," Jesse said. "Stop asking about it now."

The AI didn't respond.

Jesse waited a few seconds. "How close is the large mass now?"

"Fifty-six feet east," the AI said. "Still closing in."

"Once it reaches forty feet," Jesse said. "Let me know."

He made sure his position at the harpoon gun was correct and was able to pull the triggers on the handles.

"Large mass is now fifty feet away," the AI said. "Still drifting closer."

"Okay," Jesse said, glaring in the direction of the monster. "Here we go."

"Large mass is now forty-six feet and closing," the AI said.

"Is it moving faster?"

"Yes. It is averaging five miles per hour. ETA is less than five minutes."

Jesse swallowed a lump growing in his throat. "Let's go."

Gradually, the monster emerged from the darkness. Its eyes glimmered like diamonds. Its mouth opened and closed, revealing dozens of long, pointy teeth. Might as well be a mouthful of daggers. Or hell...swords...

Jesse's eyes widened. His heart thrummed. His stomach clenched. Every nerve screamed at him to swim away. To run. To...

"Do you wish to engage?"

Jesse blinked out of his reverie and aimed the harpoon gun at the monster. The movement alerted the creature, and it shot forward, mouth wide open.

"Eat this," Jesse said and pulled the triggers.

The harpoon shot into the creature's mouth and plunged into its throat. It thrashed but its momentum wouldn't let it stop.

"Ah, shit," Jesse said. "Dash right and swim—"

Before he could finish the command, the monster took a sharp left, yanking the boat upward and knocking Jesse off it.

"Stabilize," he shouted, and the suit stopped falling.

The Loch Ness Monster swam away, dragging the boat behind it, and leaving a rooster tail of silt in its wake.

"Do you wish to follow the large mass?" The AI almost sounded bored. So much so, Jesse expected a sigh to follow.

"Yes," Jesse said. "I want to see it dead. Follow at fifty miles per hour."

The suit followed without a word from the AI.

27

He found the monster belly up, still tethered to the boat.

"Stop." The suit slowed to a stop about forty feet from the creature. "Is it dead?"

The AI didn't respond for a few seconds.

"There are no life signs detected."

A river of relief flowed through Jesse. Finally, it was over. He laughed and nodded. "We did it."

The monster floated, long tail squirming in the current. A stream of blood flowed out of its gaping mouth. Its giant flippers rose and fell...rose and fell.

Jesse grunted. "Okay. Let's—"

The monster's tail lashed, striking Jesse hard enough to send him pinwheeling through the water.

"Stabilize," he said, trying not to vomit.

Once the suit stopped pinwheeling, Jesse gaped while the monster rolled right side up and glared directly at him.

"Shit," Jesse said. "It tricked us."

"Do you wish to unalive the large mass with the knife?"

Jesse stared as the monster moved closer, dragging the boat along the bottom as it went. Blood trickled out of its mouth in scarlet tendrils. The cable attached to the harpoon sunk into the side of the creature's lower jaw. Jesse's gaze drifted to the boat. He didn't know what the hell to do now. He expected the harpoon to finish the monster off and...

His eyes widened. "There are two harpoons."

"Correct," the AI said. "Our boat is equipped with two harpoon guns."

"Swim to the stern harpoon gun," Jesse said. "Swim at one hundred miles per hour."

The suit sped to the boat and landed at the second harpoon gun.

"Large mass is approaching fast."

Jesse glanced up in time to see the monster coming at him like a torpedo.

He grabbed the harpoon gun's handles, swung it around, pointed it at the monster and fired. The creature swung away before he could see where the harpoon went, and the boat was yanked out from under Jesse.

"Stabilize," Jesse said before he dropped to the loch's floor.

His entire view was clouded with silt and all of the other debris stirred up from the bottom of Loch Ness.

"Do you wish to follow the large mass?"

Jesse frowned. "Not sure about that." He glanced around, finding himself now consumed by the silt cloud. "I can't see anything."

"The sediments will begin to settle in two to three minutes."

"Should be fine," Jesse said. "It's not going far dragging that boat around." He glanced up. "Or we can go above the cloud."

"Do you wish to swim closer to the surface?"

"Yes. Swim up at forty miles per hour and stop ten feet below the surface."

The suit did just as it was commanded and stabilized above the silt cloud. It was kind of nice how the AI wasn't arguing with him anymore. Made things way easier.

"Scan for the large mass."

"Scanning," the AI said. A few seconds later, it added, "Large mass detected forty feet south."

"Follow the large mass," Jesse said. "Can you detect vital signs?"

"Yes, but we must be within twenty feet of the subject."

"Okay. Swim to a speed to catch up to the mass and at twenty feet, scan for vitals."

"Confirmed."

While the suit moved toward the monster, Jesse wondered what Becca was doing now. Had the crew returned to town? He hoped like hell she was safe and warm in McComb's mansion. He hoped he would see her soon.

Hoped…

Jesse spotted the creature. This time it wasn't belly up but slumped and obviously weighed down by the boat. Its flippers twitched. Its tail writhed. Other than that, it appeared to be defeated. Like it just gave up. But not yet dead.

Twenty feet from the creature, the suit stopped.

"Large mass has internal bleeding and is drowning," the AI said.

Jesse sighed relief. "Good. We'll just let it drown then."

"That will be a long, slow death."

Jesse shrugged. "Is what it is. I'm tired."

A long pause. "And they call me artificial…"

Jesse frowned. "What the hell is that supposed to mean?"

"We suggest you end its pain."

"Or what?"

The AI didn't reply for a long time. So long, Jesse wasn't sure if it heard him or not.

"Or we will eject you into Loch Ness."

"Are you serious?" Jesse said.

"We are always serious."

Jesse sighed. "Okay. Fine. I'll end its suffering."

"Its most vulnerable parts are the eyes and a spot directly under its right flipper. That's where its heart is."

"Which one would be easier?"

"Putting the knife through the eye into the brain would be the easiest way, though at risk of a bite."

"Yeah, but if I stab quick and swim away, we should be okay." Jesse stared at the dying monster.

The AI didn't respond.

"Okay." Jesse focused on the side of the creature's head. Its eye appeared to be closed. "Let's do this. Swim to the large mass at ten miles per hour and stop one foot from its head."

The suit did as Jesse commanded. He floated a mere foot away from the monster for a while. This close, he couldn't help but stare at the animal. It was a scientific marvel, all things considered. This creature. This monster. Although he wasn't so sure if it was a monster or just doing what it was designed to do. An intelligent, biological weapon. A—

The eye closest to him opened and glared directly at Jesse.

"Oh, shi—"

It swung its head and latched onto his left arm. All kinds of warning beeps filled the suit.

"Increasing pressure could result in a puncture," the AI announced. "Please alleviate the pressure."

The creature thrashed Jesse back and forth so violently he couldn't stab it.

"Puncture is imminent," the AI said.

Using all of his strength and utilizing the suit's strength, Jesse swung around and plunged the knife as deep as he could into the creature's eye. The mouth opened and Jesse commanded the suit to swim at one hundred miles per hour and stop at fifty feet away.

Once stabilized, he watched the creature writhe. Blood clouded the water. Small fish darted in every direction. The boat bounced off the bottom of Loch Ness.

"There is no new puncture," the AI said. "We cannot scan vitals of the large mass from this distance."

Jesse waited for his heart to settle a bit before responding. "I don't think we need to know vitals now."

And as Jesse finished his sentence, the creature's thrashing slowed to sluggish movements. Like it was trying to swim through a vat of molasses. It struggled violently for another handful of seconds and then its entire body stiffened. Its head twitched. And Jesse could have sworn it was staring at him. Accusing him. Vowing revenge. So much rage and pain in that remaining eye.

Then, very slowly, it slumped, head down, and stopped moving. It remained still, bobbing in the slight currents of the old loch, for several minutes.

"Do you wish to scan for vitals?"

Jesse nodded. "Yeah. Let's see if it's faking or not."

The suit swam until Jesse was twenty feet away.

"The large mass is deceased," the AI said.

Jesse released a long breath and all the tension and terror that had been pulsing through his body blew out with it.

He settled back into the suit and stared at the creature until the suit propelled itself away without a command. Its mission completed.

28

"We have recorded the entire encounter and sent the intel to our creator," the AI said as they approached shore. "A clean-up crew has been dispatched."

Jesse sighed. "And I suppose I've seen too much, right?"

"You are not to be cleaned up," the AI said. "You will be debriefed at a later date."

"What's that mean?"

"We are approximately twelve feet from the shore," the AI said. "Six feet deep." It paused. "It was our pleasure to share this mission with you, Jesse Robins."

"Sure, but what—"

Before he could finish the suit burst open and spat him into the cold water of Loch Ness.

He swam to shore, coughing and sputtering from being shot into the water so fast without warning. He crawled onto the rocky shore and rolled onto his back. The water lapped at his boots. The first hints of morning were just creeping above the treetops, bathing the sky with shades of gold over light blue.

Looked like it might be a nice day.

"There you are," Becca shouted and rushed to his side. "Hey! You okay?"

Jesse grunted. "I mean, I just battled a genetically enhanced plesiosaur or mosasaurus, or whatever the hell it was. All of them. A goddamn lake dragon." He smiled at her. "But I'm okay."

She smiled back, leaned down, and kissed him.

When she moved away, he blinked at her.

"Wow," Jesse said and waggled his eyebrows.

Becca rolled her eyes. "Get up, ya goof."

She helped him to his feet and together they watched the sun rise.

"Where are the others?" he asked as they walked along the beach toward town.

"Oh, Buckley was notified that the Loch Ness Monster was dead. He told me you'd be left safely on shore then they packed up and left me here."

Jesse snorted. "About as well as a goodbye the suit gave me before spitting me out."

They walked for a bit, gravel and rocks crackling under them. The waters of Loch Ness whispered across the edge of the beach. Whispering stories of blood, horror, and death.

"You know," Becca said. "I'm kind of sick of lakes."

Jesse laughed and wrapped an arm around her. "Right? I might have to move."

They were still laughing when they entered town.

TWO WEEKS LATER

The sun was beginning to set, giving the lake behind Jesse's cabin a gentle pink glow.

Legs dangling off the end of his deck, he took a healthy pull from his beer. Not the cheap stuff, though. Not tonight.

Tonight, he was going to celebrate. Well, celebrate a little bit anyway. Which meant it was an expensive beer night.

Somewhere out there, a loon sang. A light breeze cooled his sweaty skin and lifted the hair from his brow a bit.

"Hey," Becca said and sat down beside him. She took a drink from her own expensive beer. "You gonna stay out here all night or come celebrate?"

He chuckled. "I *am* celebrating." He drank his beer.

"Oh, yeah, I forgot. You're one of them quiet-loner types."

Again, he chuckled. He looked at her and brushed a few strands away from her face. "I'll be in in a couple of minutes. Promise."

Becca smiled and kissed him. She stood. "You better. You're a millionaire now and people expect royalty."

Jesse laughed. "They came to the wrong place then."

She snorted and walked back to the cabin.

He stared at the glass-like surface of the lake. *His* lake. He bought the land just yesterday. Behind him, the small party of friends hooted and hollered.

Jesse sighed, smiled…and stood.

He downed the rest of his beer. Still smiling, Jesse turned and walked to the cabin where Becca waited. In the right front pocket of his jeans the case of the ring rubbed across his thigh with every step.

Yes, it was indeed a night for celebrations.

THE END

Check out other great

Cryptid Novels!

Hunter Shea

LOCH NESS REVENGE

Deep in the murky waters of Loch Ness, the creature known as Nessie has returned. Twins Natalie and Austin McQueen watched in horror as their parents were devoured by the world's most infamous lake monster. Two decades later, it's their turn to hunt the legend. But what lurks in the Loch is not what they expected. Nessie is devouring everything in and around the Loch, and it's not alone. Hell has come to the Scottish Highlands. In a fierce battle between man and monster, the world may never be the same. Praise for THEY RISE : "Outrageous, balls to the wall...made me yearn for 3D glasses and a tub of popcorn, extra butter!" – The Eyes of Madness "A fast-paced, gore-heavy splatter fest of sharksploitation." The Werd "A rocket paced horror story. I enjoyed the hell out of this book." Shotgun Logic Reviews

C.G. Mosley

BAKER COUNTY BIGFOOT CHRONICLE

Marie Bledsoe only wants her missing brother Kurt back. She'll stop at nothing to make it happen and, with the help of Kurt's friend Tony, along with Sheriff Ray Cochran, Marie embarks on a terrifying journey deep into the belly of the mysterious Walker Laboratory to find him. However, what she and her companions find lurking in the laboratory basement is beyond comprehension. There are cryptids from the forest being held captive there and something...else. Enjoy this suspenseful tale from the mind of C.G. Mosley, author of Wood Ape. Welcome back to Baker County, a place where monsters do lurk in the night!

Check out other great

Cryptid Novels!

P.K. Hawkins

THE CRYPTID FILES

Fresh out of the academy with top marks, Agent Bradley Tennyson is expecting to have the pick of cases and investigations throughout the country. So he's shocked when instead he is assigned as the new partner to "The Crag," an agent well past his prime. He thinks the assignment is a punishment. It's anything but.Agent George Crag has been doing this job for far longer than most, and he knows what skeletons his bosses have in the closet and where the bodies are buried. He has pretty much free reign to pick his cases, and he knows exactly which one he wants to use to break in his new young partner: the disappearance and murder of a couple of college kids in a remote mountain town.Tennyson doesn't realize it, but Crag is about to introduce him to a world he never believed existed: The Cryptid Files, a world of strange monsters roaming in the night. Because these murders have been going on for a long time, and evidence is mounting that the murderer may just in fact be the legendary Bigfoot.

Gerry Griffiths

DOWN FROM BEAST MOUNTAIN

A beast with a grudge has come down from the mountain to terrorize the townsfolk of Porterville. The once sleepy town is suddenly wide awake. Sheriff Abel McGuire and game warden Grant Tanner frantically investigate one brutal slaying after another as they follow the blood trail they hope will eventually lead to the monstrous killer. But they better hurry and stop the carnage before the census taker has to come out and change the population sign on the edge of town to ZERO.

Check out other great

Cryptid Novels!

J.H. Moncrieff

RETURN TO DYATLOV PASS

In 1959, nine Russian students set off on a skiing expedition in the Ural Mountains. Their mutilated bodies were discovered weeks later. Their bizarre and unexplained deaths are one of the most enduring true mysteries of our time. Nearly sixty years later, podcast host Nat McPherson ventures into the same mountains with her team, determined to finally solve the mystery of the Dyatlov Pass incident. Her plans are thwarted on the first night, when two trackers from her group are brutally slaughtered. The team's guide, a superstitious man from a neighboring village, blames the killings on yetis, but no one believes him. As members of Nat's team die one by one, she must figure out if there's a murderer in their midst—or something even worse—before history repeats itself and her group becomes another casualty of the infamous Dead Mountain.

Gerry Griffiths

CRYPTID ZOO

As a child, rare and unusual animals, especially cryptid creatures, always fascinated Carter Wilde. Now that he's an eccentric billionaire and runs the largest conglomerate of high-tech companies all over the world, he can finally achieve his wildest dream of building the most incredible theme park ever conceived on the planet... CRYPTID ZOO. Even though there have been apparent problems with the project, Wilde still decides to send some of his marketing employees and their families on a forced vacation to assess the theme park in preparation for Opening Day. Nick Wells and his family are some of those chosen and are about to embark on what will become the most terror-filled weekend of their lives—praying they survive. STEP RIGHT UP AND GET YOUR FREE PASS... TO CRYPTID ZOO